# SOLOMON'S SURRENDER

MICHELLE DARE

*Paranormals of Avynwood, #4*

Cover Design by ©MaeIDesign and Photography
Photography by ©6:12 Photography by Eric McKinney
Interior Design by Down Write Nuts
Editing by Barren Acres Editing
Proofreading by Landers Editorial Services

Cocky. No word better described Solomon. He projected the playboy image, but only he knew the truth. Deep inside, he wanted what his brother and friends had—a mate.

Fifteen hundred years was a long time to be alone. Solomon's pure vampire bloodline and family name made him desirable, but that didn't take away the loneliness.

Lilah was fiercely independent and distrusting of paranormals out of necessity. Some treated her with contempt because of her half cheetah shifter/half fae heritage. They thought she was beneath them when she was actually superior.

Someone was determined to take Lilah's life, but who was behind the attacks remained a mystery. Solomon fought off the first assault then became Lilah's sole protector until he uncovered who wanted to harm her.

One wanted a mate, and the other didn't. But fate didn't ask for their opinion. They could only fight what was meant to be for so long before the inevitable happened. If they managed to stay alive, maybe they would learn what it meant to be fated.

# Dedication

To the Verascue brothers.

Ford insisted this book be dedicated to him and him alone. His reasoning was that without him, Sol wouldn't have been a part of my Avynwood world. Sol, however, said that was ridiculous. So, the book is dedicated to both of them. For without them, this world I created would be a lot less interesting.

# CHAPTER ONE

## *Solomon*

**"MORNING, SUNSHINE!"** I YELL FROM WHERE I'm perched on my deck.

Sienna jumps, almost spilling her coffee. "For the love of—! Sol, we need to work on your early morning greetings."

"It's noon, sister-in-law. If you weren't over there letting my brother devour you, you'd have caught the gorgeous sunrise this morning."

"One, I was asleep when the sun rose. And two, what Ford and I do is none of your concern."

I snort. "Keep telling yourself that."

Okay, so maybe when I paid a stupid amount of money to buy the house next to my brother in Duck, North Carolina, I should have thought about boundaries. After all, he is newly mated. Well, new meaning they've been together for a year and a half now. You'd think they'd be used to me. I'm here almost every day. I annoy them to no end and take a great amount of joy in doing so.

For as much as Ford scoffs and flips me off, he loves me. I never doubt that. And Sienna… Well, I used to hate her, then I kind of liked her, now I love her. She's family, even though she hasn't fully embraced being a Verascue yet. She should, though. We're freaking awesome.

"What do you have planned for the day?" she asks as she settles into one of those anti-gravity lounge chairs. I'm not sure how she does it without spilling her drink. Every time I sit in one of them, it either feels like I'm going to go butt over head backward, or I get folded up in it and want to shred it into a million pieces. Sienna gets into it with grace and has no problems. I'll stick to lounging on the deck railing nearest their home.

"Oh, a little of this, a little of that," I reply.

The waves crash on shore on the other side of the sand dunes in front of our homes. There's a high rip current threat today. The ocean is rough, yet there are still people out there in it. Days like this make me nervous. Not for myself, but for the humans who've decided to go in the ocean when they aren't very strong swimmers. Any time this threat is there, swimmers should be cautious. I've seen and rescued people from drowning. The ocean is unpredictable. It doesn't care what age you are or where you're from. It will suck you under and churn you around until you're fighting to breach the surface.

Hence, why I'm out here. With my great hearing, I can immediately hear any shouts for help and run out there to assist. I helped someone yesterday. Their family asked for my name. I shook my head and told them I just wanted to help. They hugged me and thanked me. Rescuing their family member was the least I could. To have the abilities I and so many other paranormals do, we should be out there helping in any way we can. Creating a more peaceful world. Not making it a worse place.

Sure, I run my mouth with the best of them, but this is my town—mine and my family's. We live here almost year-round. We never want to see anyone hurt or worse. I can't tell you how many times Ford and I have shown up when needed on the shoreline. I was even asked if I wanted to be a lifeguard. I politely declined, although, I'd make those red shorts look good.

The sliding door to my brother's home opens and he comes strolling out, shutting it behind him. Today he's wearing a pair of slate blue shorts and a white T-shirt. Everyone else loves seeing Ford dressed summer casual. Not in his leather trench that he thinks makes him look like a bad boy.

"Not think, brother," he says, reading my mind. "Does. No one looks as good in leather as I do." I don't bother throwing a block up in my head. There's not much in there I don't want Ford to know about. Just some properties I have stashed around the world and some emotions I lock down with four padlocks inside a heavy-duty safe even my mother can't get into.

As far as the properties go, I like to keep parts of my life private. I like that I can go somewhere no one can find me. I love my family, but sometimes I need a break. One where I can sit and think without interruption. A place where I won't get unexpected visitors teleporting inside.

"You can go inside, Sol. I've got it out here for a bit," Ford says, aware of the exact reason why I'm sitting here.

"Thanks, brother." The nights are calmer with almost everyone inside, but the summer days, there are a lot of tourists out and about.

I slip off the railing and go inside my home. It's not set

up the same as Ford's but blends in nicely along the coast. You won't see huge high-rises on the shoreline here. There are resorts, hotels, and homes. A lot of the people who own here rent their homes out over the summer.

With the door shut behind me, I try to think about what I want to do today. I really need to go to the grocery store. I could order and have it delivered, but there's no fun in that. There's no way to know what kind of hot female I'm going to find in the store. This time of year, it's like a buffet when I enter. The bright lights of the store shine down on all the gorgeous females, highlighting their curves.

I'm not a total jerk, though. I stay away from families and anyone married. But the single females, I'm there.

Grabbing my keys, I head downstairs to my garage and my baby. Not an actual baby, but she was expensive enough that I call her one. When I bought this house, I needed a car. I got tired of driving Ford's Audi when I needed to go somewhere.

I step down onto the concrete floor and take her in. Four doors, V-twelve under the hood, and painted in Scintilla Silver. The Aston Martin Rapide AMR is one fine looking car.

Opening the door, I slip onto the buttery soft seat that cradles me perfectly and open the garage door. Maybe I'll just cruise around for a bit. I'll open the windows, let some music play. It'll be a great day.

I back out of the garage and turn the car around before closing the door. The road I live on is quiet today. No doubt everyone is enjoying the beach or one of the many activities the Outer Banks offers.

"Oh, come on," I say to myself.

At the end of my street is nothing but solid traffic. And here I thought I'd have fun today going to the store. It's then I remember it's Saturday—one of the popular check-in, check-out days here on the barrier islands. I should have thought this through.

Someone in a tan sedan waves me out so I can slip into traffic and stop fifty feet from the end of my road. Joy. As much as I love it here, I could do without the bumper-to-bumper cars every weekend during peak season. I turn on the music and roll down the windows to let the salty fresh air in, along with a healthy dose of heat, but I'm used to that.

A group of males in front of me in a topless Jeep start blasting rock so loud it drowns out my own. Yup, should have stayed home. I watch as they whistle at a passing car of females. It's taking everything in me not to get out and knock them down a notch—cocky humans. I'm cocky, but I'm fantastic. Them… No. You don't whistle and catcall at females. They should have more respect for them than that.

We slowly move down the road until we reach the point where I can turn and head toward one of the bigger grocery stores. There is a local one near me that I love to pick up dessert from, however it's not big enough for a full shop. Yes, I have a sweet tooth. Don't judge. I like all kinds of food.

Finally, I make it to the store and park at the end of one of the aisles. I don't need anyone dinging my baby with their car door or stray cart they couldn't put away. Twenty minutes later, I'm moving up and down the aisles like a normal person. Except I'm not. I'm a vampire, out in broad daylight, shopping for the essentials. You know, candy, meat, chips, etcetera. None of that lettuce and other things. Sienna tries enough for ten paranormals to shove organic vegetables and fruit down my throat. When it's just me, I live it up.

I grab a particularly good-looking steak and put it in my half full cart.

"Quite a selection you got there," a female purrs behind me. Turning, I find a slender blonde with shorts barely covering her butt and legs that go on for days. *Well, hello there.*

"I like to live on the edge," I tell her and flash her the signature Verascue smirk.

"Nothing wrong with a little excitement."

"Oh, darling, you're barking up the right tree, then. What do you say we shop together and get to know each other in aisles four through ten?"

She smiles. White, straight teeth, soft pink lip gloss. Yup, she's mine tonight. "I'd like that."

Together, we go up and down the aisles, me throwing random stuff into the cart because I can't keep my eyes from roving over every square inch of her body. No one could blame me when she bends over to pick something up off a low shelf. I don't have a clue what it is, nor do I care. She can bend over like that back at my house tonight with nothing on. Okay, I'm a total pig. I can't help it. I love the female form.

"Solomon, honestly," a woman's voice says behind me, and I instantly still. I know that voice all too well. Turning slowly, I come face-to-face with none other than my mom.

Eloise Verascue stands behind me next to the hot dog rolls with her arms crossed and an eyebrow quirked. "Care to tell me why you're slumming it when you could be in Italy?"

"You have a house in Italy?" the female beside me speaks up with unrestrained awe in her voice. Oh, no. This isn't going to be good.

"Run along, little one," my mom says. "You won't be

my son's plaything tonight."

"Plaything?" she asks, shocked. Rightfully so. My mom isn't exactly subtle.

"Please, did you really think you were up to par for a fine specimen like him? Look at yourself."

"He's dressed like I am," the female says as she points at me.

"No, he's not. There's no part of him that's barely covered. He's dressed as he should be. You, however, look like you're about to dance against a pole. Besides that, his car probably costs more than your house, so move along." She actually shoos her with her hand.

I groan and turn to the female who is all kinds of irritated. "Sorry, darling. Maybe another time."

She flips her hair over her shoulder. "That's never going to happen." Then she stomps away.

I glare at my mom. "Was that necessary?"

"When are you going to get your life together and stop preying on tourists?"

"That's what you and father do in Italy!" I instantly realize I just yelled way too loudly and drop my voice. "You're a hypocrite."

"I'm your mother and I want grandchildren. Ford and his mate aren't there yet, so I'm depending on you."

"I'm not even ma—" I stop myself before I say mated. "Married and you're already pushing me for children? You've lost your mind, female."

"We'll see."

"Why are you here anyway?" I ask and continue with my grocery shopping. I look down into my cart. When did I throw a frying pan in there? I pick it up and put it on the nearest shelf.

"I came to visit your brother and he told me you went

shopping, so I figured I'd join you and prevent you from making your nightly mistake. You can only drown your feelings for so long, Solomon. You need to find your mate." I'm so not in the mood for this conversation.

"What do you think I've been doing for the last fifteen hundred years?" I hiss low.

"You've been screwing every unattached female you come across, paranormal or otherwise."

A man in a white shirt, cargo shorts, and sandals eyes us as my mom says the word paranormal. That's right, keep walking. Nothing to see here. Certainly not two vampires looking at sundae toppings.

"Can the lecture wait until we're back at my house?" I ask.

She sighs. "Fine. Whatever. But we're talking about this then we're going over to your brother's for dinner. Grab another steak. Your father is there, too. You know how ravenous he gets."

*Somebody save me.*

# CHAPTER TWO

## *Lilah*

**WHAT IN THE FRESH HELL** DID I JUST STEP INTO?

"Constance! So glad you're here!" Jocelyn, one of the waitresses, rushes over to me. Her cropped purple hair falls into her eyes when she stops in front of me. She blows out a bit of air to move it.

"What happened?"

"Donovon got a little rough."

"A little?"

I'm two feet into the bar and there are four large, burly men sprawled out on the floor in front of me. The lights are dim, the other patrons pressed to the walls, not wanting to get mixed up in whatever happened. And amidst it all is a very angry bear shifter in his human form.

"Don," I say carefully as I approach. "What happened?"

He's seething, his chest rising and falling rapidly. "It wasn't me. I didn't start it. It was him. Always him." Well, that explains it.

I glance down to my left and there, with his face about two inches from my black high heel, is Don's brother,

Alton. His nose is broken, blood puddled underneath it, and his eye is swelling nicely.

"I can't deal with him, Constance. I just can't." Everyone, and I mean everyone, calls me Constance. It's my middle name—the one I go by. Lilah is the name my father gave me. The male who couldn't stand to raise me, and bailed, but had enough sense to give me my mother's name as my middle name. So that's what I use when I introduce myself to people.

"Help me get them up."

Don bends down and grabs the guy closest to him by the arm, lifts him, then tosses him over his shoulder effortlessly. I do the same with Alton and try not to notice everyone's eyes on me. It's not every day a five foot nine inch female in black stilettos hauls a two hundred and fifty-pound man of pure muscle over her shoulder like he weighs nothing. If only the humans knew I'm not the average female.

I follow Don down the hallway to the back door where he pushes it open and launches the man into the employee parking lot behind the bar. His face comes into my view.

"Isn't that your cousin?" I ask.

"Not anymore," he growls. "Give me my brother."

I spin as he reaches for him and toss Alton next to Samuel on the ground. "No, you've done enough damage. Once we get the other two out here, I'm going to perform a little magic and wake them up. They need to shift to heal."

"They could die out here for all I care."

I sigh and look at the man who I've called my best friend for the past two years. His warm brown hair is getting long, the front falling over his face, reaching his chin where he has a short beard. Blood is smeared on the corner of his eye and drips from his knuckles.

Stepping over to him, I brush his hair out of the way and use a little magic to clean him up. Not to heal him but to make him look like he wasn't just in a knockdown, drag out that I missed. "You can't keep doing this."

His eyes meet mine and in them is so much pain. My heart breaks for him. "He came to apologize. Told me our parents wanted to see me again."

"That's a good thing. But I don't get why you hit him."

"He's the new alpha."

"No!" I gasp in shock.

Don was the first son his parents had. He was the one who was supposed to become alpha when his dad died or decided he didn't want the title anymore. But Don was kicked out of the clan when he was two hundred years old.

"It was supposed to be me," he says.

"You didn't want to be alpha, though. You made a decision and stuck with it."

"I couldn't stay and you know that. Winny left and I followed. Everyone hated her. Even though she left me behind so she could live with her mate." This is such a colossal mess. I can't even believe all that's going on.

"Winny was your best friend. Of course you followed her. You were supportive and she was the only one you could trust after that." I decide not to bring up how she killed Don's sister.

It was a justified challenge over a male. They fought to the death and Winny won. But when you kill the alpha's child, regardless of it being justified or not, there was no returning to that clan.

Don pleaded her case, knowing any other alpha would side with who won the challenge. Shifters fight to the death all the time. But his father blamed him. Told him if he would have kept Winny in line, it would never have gotten that far. That if he were a real alpha in training, he would have put a stop to it. Don was ultimately blamed for his sister's death.

That's where I come in. I met him at his lowest moment after he'd been on his own for ten years, roaming around North Carolina.

"Hey, guys," Jocelyn says as she peeks her head out the door. "Sorry to interrupt, but the other two are starting to wake."

"Right," Donovon says and puts his mask of indifference back into place. We both go inside and bring the other two out to the parking lot. Don kicks the door shut to be sure no one witnesses me using my magic to wake them. Luckily, it's dark; night already fell.

"You going inside?" I ask him.

He crosses his arms. "I'm not leaving you out here with them."

"Fine. Whatever." He's itching to keep fighting, but I can't let him. He has a bar to run.

Using my magic, I pour just enough into it to rouse the men. They're not so severely hurt they can't wake up. They're just knocked out cold.

One by one they rouse, but it isn't until Alton realizes what's going on that he's on his feet, eyes flashing ruby red as his bear rises to the surface. Bears are some of the scariest shifters out there. Those red eyes alone are enough to be intimidating.

I put myself between Alton and Don. "Al, you need to calm down."

"Out of the way, Constance. This doesn't pertain to you."

"That's a lie. Anything involving Don pertains to me."

His eyes go back to the amber I'm used to as he peers

down at me. Al and Don both easily have seven inches on me. "Con, this isn't your fight. Besides, I apologized and he still decked me."

"That's because you're alpha. You had to know he wasn't going to take that well."

"He wasn't there to claim it!" he yells, his voice rising rapidly.

"Was he even considered?"

"Well, no, but that's not the point."

"It is," I say calmly, knowing these males will feed off my energy if I get too wound up. "Don is as much an alpha as you are. If your parents were smart, they would have asked him first, regardless of where he currently lives. Regardless of what happened. That clan is as much his as it is yours."

"He wouldn't have taken it," Al states, anger leaving him.

Don shows a brief moment of insecurity and toes a few rocks on the ground with the tip of his black boot. "I didn't want it. Although, I wasn't asked. I'm still no one to them." And there we have it: the root cause of this. He wants his parents to see the mistake they made when they kicked him out of the clan. He wants to be accepted back in.

"They want you to come back," Al says.

Don raises his eyes to meet his brother's. "Why?" Al freezes, his tongue tied, but Don knows. "They don't want me back, do they?"

Al finally gathers his bearings and throws his hands up in the air. "Fine, they don't, but I do!"

"And then what? I'm supposed to be your beta or something? That would never happen."

"No, but you could be my brother. You could be part of the clan. I miss you, Don."

Don shakes his head in resignation. "I can't do this. You stood by them when they threw me out. You didn't fight for me. You knew Winny was justified, even if it was our sister who lost her life, yet I'm supposed to believe this now? What changed?"

Al reaches over to his right and pulls a male with dark blond hair, and the most beautiful crystal blue eyes I've ever seen, to his side. "I'd like to introduce you to my mate."

"What?" Don and I yell in unison. I didn't even know he was interested in anyone. Every time I've seen Al, he's been alone.

"Lorne is my fated mate. He came to the clan a few months ago and we got to know each other. One night we were on patrol and got to talking. Next thing we knew, our hands touched on accident and the rest is history." Al looks over at his mate and their eyes meet. So much love is between them it's almost palpable. And joy. I love seeing him like this.

"Oh, Al. I'm so happy for you," I say and step forward to hug him. "Welcome to the craziness, Lorne." I embrace him, too.

"Conni!" Don yells. "You're just going to forget what I went through?"

I turn back to Don and walk over to him. Cupping his cheeks, I bring his face down to mine, only a few inches apart. I don't desire him. But in him I've found a sense of family.

"Stop for one second," I tell him. "Look at what's going on. Your brother is mated. He's happy. Can we celebrate that?"

"He took what was mine."

"You didn't want it."

"I wanted the option."

"Do we need to talk about us not always getting our way?" This isn't the first time I've spoken to him as if he were a child, and I doubt it will be the last.

His lips lift on one side in a small smile. "How do you always do that? You manage to defuse any situation."

"I don't like you fighting with your family. You can be big and tough all you want, but you miss your brother."

He sighs. "Fine. You're right." I nod and release him. Don steps around me and stops in front of Alton. I don't miss the way Lorne tenses by his side, ready to jump in if things go downhill again. "At ease, Lorne. I'm done fighting. I'm happy for you, little brother. Not about the alpha thing but about your mate. I want you to live a full, rich life."

Al lets out a long breath and the tension eases in his shoulders. "I was worried you wouldn't be okay with me being gay."

"Are you serious?" Don asks incredulously. "I don't care who you love. I wish you would have told me sooner. I would have been there for you. I do, however, care that you became alpha behind my back."

"I didn't have much choice."

Don's brows furrow. "What do you mean?"

"Dad isn't doing well. I need you to come home."

"Why didn't you lead with that?" Donovon yells. "Holy fate, Al!"

Don turns to me and opens his mouth, but I cut him off. "I got this. Go. Be with your family. I'll take care of things here."

"Are you sure?"

"Absolutely." Not at all, but I want Don to be there when his family needs him. He's been messed up over this for years. Maybe he can finally make peace with everything.

“Thanks, Conni,” he says and hugs me tight. Then Al and Lorne do the same. The other two males blend into the background as I make my way inside.

Jocelyn mops the floor as Justin, the bartender, rights the tables and chairs that were knocked over in the fight. There’s a low chatter as people take their seats. If they only knew they almost had a full-on shifter fight on their hands, they wouldn’t still be here. However, they have no clue and Don prefers to keep it that way. Jocelyn and Justin are both humans who are very aware of our world.

Justin makes his way back behind the bar and I offer him a small smile. “Thanks for that.”

“No problem. I knew you had to handle things out back.”

“Guess it’s just the three of us. Don has to head home for a bit.”

“We’ve got it.”

I nod. We don’t have a choice.

About an hour later, Don is gone. I’m pouring a drink for one of the tables when the door to the bar opens and a tall muscular male walks in. He’s not human. I can tell by the way he carries himself with the utmost confidence. It’s difficult to pinpoint what he is.

He looks around; his grey eyes bright even in the low lighting. He has light blond hair that’s cut close on the sides and back, a little longer on top. Even though he’s dressed casually, he seems out of place here. Like he’d fit in better at a fancy restaurant. Not that this place is awful. It’s clean and sees a lot of regulars and tourists, but there’s this air about the male. Sophistication.

Then he spots me. It’s like I’m a bug caught in a spider’s web. I can’t move. I’m frozen where I stand—ensnared by the paranormal in the bar.

He walks over, drops down on the barstool in front of me, and smiles. "Looks like I picked the right bar to grab a drink. What are you doing tonight?" Just like that, the spell breaks, and I realize he's like the other low-life males out there with one thing on their minds.

"Not you," I reply sharply.

# CHAPTER THREE

*Solomon*

**I LAUGH LOUDLY AT** HER REPLY. OH, SHE'S going to be a lot of fun. Now I have to have her. The chase is on.

"Come on. Don't be like that. I wasn't asking you to come back to my place. Just what you had planned after your shift is over."

She quirks an eyebrow at me. Her long, brown hair is pulled up into a high ponytail. The shirt she's wearing reads, "Grizzly Don's Tavern" and there is a bear drinking a mug of beer. There's no doubt in my mind that this place is run by a bear shifter. The beauty in front of me is also a paranormal, though I don't get the bear vibe from her. She's something else, however, I'm not sure what.

She watches me with a hard glare. "What I do when I leave here is none of your business. I'm not interested." I take a quick moment to look through her mind until I find her name in there. I don't look for anything else. While normally I don't care about going into someone's head and seeing what's up, she's different. I'm not sure what to do with that thought, so I focus back on her with the goal to get to know her better.

She turns and goes to work mixing a drink for the waitress standing near the bar.

"What about a date?" I ask. She ignores me. "Lilah, I know you can hear me."

She freezes, her body going completely rigid. I don't miss the sharp intake of breath from the waitress nearby. Slowly, Lilah turns, drink still in hand, and walks back over until she's standing in front of me.

I pluck the half-full glass out of her hand and take a healthy swallow. No, it won't get me drunk, not even tipsy. This is all so I can get under her skin. Or in her bed. Whichever. "Thanks, but I haven't ordered anything yet."

Through clenched teeth she seethes, "Don't ever call me that again." Her voice drops to a whisper. "And don't ever go into my head again. What's in there is none of your business."

"Everything is my business, darling."

She lifts her arm and points to the door. "Out. Get out of here before I remove you."

I lean back slightly and cross my arms. "I'd like to see you try."

Another bartender comes over. His physique screams ex-military, but he's human. I could take him down without breaking a sweat. What surprises me is that he doesn't offer to fight me on Lilah's behalf. Instead, he says, "Take care of him. I got this."

Lilah nods and walks around the bar until she's standing before me. And oh, what a view it is. Her shirt is tucked into very short black shorts. Her legs are long and slender yet toned. And holy fate, those heels. They show off her calves nicely.

Once my gaze makes its way up to her face, I notice the steely look she's giving me. "About done?" she asks.

"Not even close."

"Come with me." She nods toward the hallway leading to the back.

"With pleasure."

So this is how it's going to go? She's going to take me in the back and have her way with me on one of the desks or maybe up against a wall. I could totally get on board with that.

Once we're out of view and earshot of the patrons, she spins and slams me hard into the wall, her hand fisting my shirt. Her voice enters my mind. *"I want you out of this bar. You're never to come back."*

*"Well, well, well, you're full of secrets, aren't you? I should have taken a longer stroll in your head. What are you exactly?"* I still haven't got a clue. I'm getting a fae or vampire vibe. Unless she's something else and a vampire transferred powers to her.

*"What I am is not interested."*

*"I beg to differ. I can hear your rapid breaths, Lilah. I can hear the rush of your blood through your veins. Your heart is beating fast and your pupils are dilated."* My fangs descend on their own accord, but I keep them concealed with my mouth closed in case someone should walk back here.

*"Listen, vampire, I want you gone. I'm not in the mood for your games."*

*"Mood? No, obviously not. But you can't lie to me when I can clearly see the tells your body is giving me."*

She shoves me hard then releases me, stalking down the hall and out the back door. It slams into the wall. I follow her, of course. I mean, at this point I'm completely invested. She's putting up a great fight. Beyond the desire to have my fangs in her neck, I want to get to know her.

I stop short. What's going on? I don't normally want

to get to know anyone. I really need to get my head back in the game. This is not typical behavior for me.

I start walking again and am in the back parking lot of the bar, where I find her leaning against the wall. "I really rattled you, huh?" I ask.

"I don't like paranormals in my head," she all but growls.

"I don't like being thrust against the wall unless my partner and me are both naked, yet that's exactly what you did to me."

"How did you even get in my head? I have a block set up by a mage."

"Please." Then it occurs to me, she doesn't know who I am. Seems I'm not spreading enough stories around about my family and me. Everyone should know the Verascues. We're legendary. "I'm a Verascue, darling. I do as I please."

She cocks her head slightly. "I've never heard your name, nor do I care about your game. You could be the vampire king and I'd want you away from me."

I step closer. "I'm not going anywhere."

Her hands flatten on the wall at her back. "Don't you dare come closer," she hisses and her eyes flash from brown to sapphire.

"Oh, we're a cat, are we?" That's unexpected.

Pushing off the wall, she's only inches from me. This time I'm keenly aware of her scent. Lavender mixed with beer and the greasy smell of food that permeates the air in the bar. "What I am is none of your business. You're going to leave this area and not come back."

I scoff. "Not likely. I live in Duck. Your bar isn't far from where I reside. I think I'll come here every night."

"Then you'll be met with a wall of bear shifters."

My eyes brighten as excitement flows through me.

"That sounds fantastic! I'll bring a pack of wolves and my other paranormal friends. We'll have a rumble. And then, when we win—because we always win—I'll get to take you on a date, and you'll tell me all about yourself."

"Are you always this cocky?"

"Yes," I reply, completely serious.

"I'm never going to do anything with you. And like I said, I have an entire clan of bears at my back."

"Yet, you're out here all alone." This is a tease. She wants me. At least her body does. Her mind isn't on board yet, but it will be. I'm irresistible. "I'm going to leave… For now. But I will be back. If I encounter a wall of grizzly then I'll teleport away and be back with a wall of wolves. I don't give up on what I want. I always get my way."

"Get used to disappointment. You've never met anyone like me." She's got that right.

She leans in, like she's taking my scent into her very being and her eyes flash sapphire again. I love how they stand out, even in the dark. Not only have I piqued her interest, but her cat's as well. And not in the *I'm going to rip out your throat* kind of way. If she wanted to shift and shred me, she would have.

"See you around, kitten," I toss over my shoulder as I turn and leave.

If she won't give in tonight, she will eventually. I could feel the heat coming off of her. She can deny her reaction to me until she's blue in the face. But her desire—her animal—she doesn't lie. They want me. Eventually, she'll give up the fight. Until then, I'm going to make this place my nightly hangout. I'll sit and drink. Every time she sees me, she'll remember what it felt like to be close to me. The way my voice caressed her skin. How her body pulsed with desire when I was near.

I try to pretend I'm completely unaffected as I climb into my car and pull out onto the road. I try to put her scent, her long legs, and her grace out of my head as I drive north to my home. None of it does me any good.

It's not until I'm home, lying in bed with sounds of the ocean as my backdrop, that I finally give in and go over the reasons why she was so intriguing. She still is. She's a cat, but which one? I can picture her as so many. And I can't forget that she can speak via telepathy. So has she been bitten? Has another vampire sunk their fangs into her and drank her delicious blood? The thought of another male's teeth in her causes fury to flow through me.

I sit up and scrub my hands over my face. What's going on here?

Quickly, I teleport to the deck of my brother's home and listen. I've interrupted them on far too many occasions by not thinking before teleporting over. For all our sanity, I listen first now.

The television is on and I can hear their conversation about whatever they're watching. Good, no drinking, cuddling, or anything more.

With a snap, I teleport into their upstairs seating area and stand between them and the television.

"Why, brother, it's so nice to see you. Again," Ford says dryly. I was here this morning. I got bored and was fearful if I went out, Mom would show up. I couldn't think of anything else to do, so I bothered my brother.

"I have a problem," I state.

Ford sits up straight, his arm slipping from Sienna's shoulders where she's tucked against him. A murderous rage flashes on his face as his fangs descend. "Who do I have to kill?" I love my brother for a lot of reasons, but this is one of the main ones. No matter the difference in our ages, or how many fights we had while he was growing up, he's quick to come to my defense and I'm the same with him.

"No one needs to be killed. Well, not yet anyway. I might have a bunch of bears to fight. That's not immediate, though." I rattle on, barely taking time to suck in a breath in between sentences. "I met a female and can't get her out of my head." There, I said it.

A slow smile spreads over Ford's face as Sienna beams. "I'm so happy for you!" she yells and jumps up to hug me.

I grip her gently by the shoulders to hold her at bay. "Hold on, female. I didn't say I found my mate. Just someone who intrigues me and I'm not sure what to do about it."

"Sol," Sienna says, her eyes holding mine. "We know better than anyone else that no female has ever gotten you riled up. You rarely talk about the ones you bring home or visit. So, regardless of what you tell yourself about this female, there's something special about her."

Ford stands and comes over to clasp me on the shoulder. "It's a big day, brother." He smiles wide. "I'm so glad I'm here to witness it."

# CHAPTER FOUR

## *Lilah*

**"HOW ARE THINGS AT** THE BAR?" DON ASKS over the phone. It's only been twenty-four hours since he left, but the bar is his baby. I'm honestly surprised he didn't check in before this.

"It's fine. Don't worry about it. How's your dad?"

"He's not going to make it much longer. I could tell he was happy to see me, but he can barely talk. He's a thousand and fifteen. It's his time. I just wish it didn't take him dying for us to make amends."

"I'm so sorry. Do you know what you're going to do? Are you going to stay there or come back here?" Nerves flitter through me at the thought of not having Don around anymore. Him, this bar, they've been my home. Even as I look around the horrible wood paneling of his office, all I can think about is how I'd feel if I didn't work here anymore.

Not only has Don been like family to me, but he also let me crash here when I had nowhere to stay. There's still a bed in the room across the hall. He said he didn't want to get rid of it in case someone else came through and needed a place to sleep. Don has one of the biggest hearts I've ever seen.

"I'm not coming back here permanently, Conni. Don't worry about that. Alton has the clan handled. I'm not their alpha and the more I see of the others, the more I realize this isn't my home anymore." I let out a breath as the tension drains from my shoulders. "I'm not abandoning you. Please understand that." In the amount of time we've been friends, he's learned everything about me. Though I might not speak about my issues, Donovon knows them better than anyone.

"Thank you," I say weakly. I might have a tough exterior, but inside I feel everything. I've just learned over the years that it's better not to show emotion. That doing so leaves me vulnerable, and I never want to be that again.

"Has it been busy?" he asks. I appreciate the change of subject.

"So-so. Though there was this vampire who came in and tried to pick me up. Too bad he had a strong block up and I couldn't read his mind."

Don laughs. "When isn't there someone in there trying to pick you up?"

I roll my eyes, even though he can't see me. "I know, but this male was different. Persistent as all get out. He brought up his family name like it meant something to me, which it absolutely didn't. I'd never heard it before."

"What was his name?"

"Verascue, I think, was his last name."

"What?" Don yells. "You had one of the Verascues in the bar and gave him grief?"

"He was being pushy," I reply haughtily.

"Did he put his hands on you?" Don growls low. I have no doubt his bear rose to the surface.

"No, I pushed him into the wall, but I didn't let our skin touch and he never once reached out for me."

"Okay, so let me get this straight," he says calmer. "One of the males from what has to be the most prominent vampire family on the planet came into the bar, hit on you, didn't lay one finger on you, and you got rough with him?"

"That's about right. Although, I'm not sure about him being from a prominent family."

"What am I going to do with you, Conni? This could be really big for business. I knew the brothers lived on the Outer Banks, but I had no idea where. We could use the kind of publicity they could bring to the bar."

"There's two of them?" Great. Just what I need.

"Yes. I think Ford is mated, which means it was Solomon who came into the bar."

"He's not a celebrity," I scoff.

"Oh, but he is. You haven't been around long enough, however, those of us who have are aware you don't screw with that family. They fought in the pack war that happened recently. I'm sure you've heard of that."

"Yeah, I remember you talking about it after it happened."

"I was away at the time and you were holding down the bar. I didn't want you involved, so I didn't bring it up until after it happened and I was back. The four members of the Verascue family fought alongside the Avynwood Pack. They're a formidable force."

"Whatever they are, I'm not going to sit here and let him hit on me when I'm not interested."

There's a long pause before Don speaks up again. "It's not a bad thing to date someone."

"Can we not start this again? I'm young and have zero interest in having a mate." Don's heart is in the right place, but I don't want to be bound to one male. No way. No how. Not going to happen.

"The Verascues could offer you protection like no other. Might not be a bad idea to get on their good side." I can't believe this male.

"So you want me to whore myself out so I can have more protection? Last I checked, I can take care of myself and, when I can't, I have you."

"Now hold on a minute. I never said to whore yourself out. I'm only saying to give it a chance. In the time I've known you, I've never seen you on one date."

"Maybe because I don't need a male to be happy."

"But are you, Conni? Happy?" He has me there and knows it.

"I've gotta go."

"You're avoiding the conversation."

"I'm ending the conversation. I love you, but I'm not in the mood for this. The more you push, the more I'll withdraw. You know this about me."

"I do, but I was hoping you'd take a leap, even if this vampire turns out to be nothing but a friend. We could always use more of those. You don't understand the importance of strong allies. If anything happens, having someone you can count on to have your back can mean the difference between life and death. I'd fight until my dying breath for you, but there's only me. My clan isn't local and they aren't even mine. They're Alton's now. Just think about it. You need more than me, Conni. You need to get out there. There's so much to see and do. Leave North Carolina. Travel. You'd be surprised what you see." He has very valid points. That doesn't mean I have to take his advice. I'm fine with my life the way it is.

"And what about you? I'm just supposed to quit the

bar? You don't need me?" I fight down the emotion rising in my throat. He's all I have here, and at the moment, it feels like he's pushing me away.

"I'll be fine." He sighs. "Listen, I know how much you hate being told what to do, so I'll leave it at this. Stay, go, whatever. At the end of the day, all that matters is your happiness. If that means you spend four days out of every week in my bar serving drinks, then so be it. But if it means you get to see the world, with or without this vampire, then I'll cheer you on every step of the way. Happiness, Constance. That's all I want for you."

I sniffle, fighting back tears at his kind words. "Why couldn't you have been my mate?" I remember thinking he was attractive when we first met. I mean, how could I not? He's the ultimate sexy shifter with his rugged good looks. Plus, he's a freaking bear. The raw power residing in him is a huge turn-on. But the second our hands touched, I knew he wasn't mine. Nevertheless, he's had my back every day since.

Donovon laughs. "You couldn't handle me."

"I think it's the other way around."

"You're probably right."

We talk a few minutes more about the delivery he's waiting for before ending the call. It should be here tomorrow morning. I'll handle it. He makes me promise I won't close the bar alone. Even though I can take care of myself, he doesn't like the idea of me on my own and something happening.

Donovon won't be back until his dad passes away, which could be tomorrow or a month from now. No way to tell. He did say he was going to send a friend over tonight to help out at the bar. While I love Justin and Jocelyn, if it gets too busy, we'll need the extra help.

I spend a little while organizing Don's desk, because let's face it, the male is not known for his organizational skills. Afterward, I make my way back out front and find a packed bar and half the tables filled. How long was I on the phone?

I step behind the bar and jump into the fray filling orders. Justin and I work seamlessly, moving around each other, never bumping into one another. Justin is a good guy, but like Don, no sparks, which is a good thing. I don't want a mate.

The door opens and a tall male comes through. His hair is shockingly white and cut in a mohawk. But instead of it sticking up on the top, it falls over to one side. He's muscular but lean. Definitely not a bear shifter, but he's something paranormal for sure.

He catches my gaze and instantly smiles as he walks over to the bar. "You must be Constance," he greets with an outstretched hand.

I'm always reluctant to shake hands, or have any kind of contact with anyone, never knowing who's going to end up being my mate. But I can't be rude, so I steel myself and take his hand in mine to shake it. No sparks. Thank fate for that.

"I am," I smile. "You must be the friend Don sent over."

"That's me. I'm Tristin. It's nice to meet you."

"Same. So, what can you do?" I'm going to throw him right into work. If he's here thanks to Don, then he's going to earn his keep.

"I can mix drinks, or I can wait tables. Whatever you like."

I glance around the bar and see the mostly male clientele. "How about you help Jocelyn out tonight with the tables, then help me stock the bar when we close."

"Sounds good."

Bringing him into the back, I find a new T-shirt with the bar's logo on the front and hand it to him. I also give him a pad to take orders on. He could have a great memory, but at least this way he can use the pad if he wants.

He plucks one of the pens off the desk and tucks it behind his ear. I go through the food menu with him, which is short and to the point. We don't offer a lot. The cook is only here after four in the afternoon and with the limited menu, it's hard to screw things up.

Tristin goes on his way, and within the hour, we're all in a good groove and the bar is full. Money changes hands, drinks are served, food is plated; it's a great, busy night.

That is until a certain vampire shows up again and I sigh loud enough to draw Justin's attention.

He gently elbows me in the side. "You like him."

"What?" I spin with wide eyes.

"Any other guy who hits on you gets next to no attention from you. This guy," he nods toward the male who sits down about four places up the bar. "He does something to you."

"Yeah, he lights a rage under my skin."

"I don't think it's rage." He winks, then just so happens to walk to the opposite end of the bar, completely ignoring the male who sat down.

Lovely. Now Justin is trying to set me up. As if it weren't bad enough to have Don on me about this. Maybe Jocelyn and Tristin can gang up on me and push me into the vampire's lap, where I'll let him suck on my neck. Not. Gonna. Happen.

I finish getting another beer for the male in front of me before walking down to see what the vampire wants.

"Solomon," he says, holding my eyes. "Not the vampire. Solomon."

"Get out of my head," I growl. I knew his name. Don told me, but he's still the vampire to me.

"I wasn't in your head, kitten. Your thoughts floated right to me. It's nice to see I take up so much space in that pretty little head of yours." He smirks.

I remember Don's words about having friends and allies. It's the only reason I grit my teeth and ask, "What can I get you?"

Solomon leans forward, resting his elbows on top of the bar and smiles. "That was hard for you, wasn't it?"

"Oh, forget this." I turn to walk back to where I was, but his hand shoots out to hook in one of the belt loops of my shorts. He pulls me to a stop. Glancing down at his hand, I slowly raise my gaze to meet his. "Hands off me, leech."

# CHAPTER FIVE

## *Solomon*

**OH, HOW I LOVE A** FEISTY FEMALE. I barely touched her, and she's got fire in her eyes.

She jerks out of my grasp. Luckily, I released her or her shorts would have ripped where I held them. If I hadn't been aware of the blatant desire running through her veins last night, I wouldn't be so forward today. The last thing I want to do is chase a female who doesn't want me. But Lilah does, even if she won't admit it.

"What do you want to drink?" she grates out. This is so much fun.

"A water, please."

"Water? You seriously came down to the bar for freaking water?"

"Well, you and I both know that alcohol has zero effect on me, and unless you have some wine back there, water it is." They could have fae wine behind the bar. It's not like I could say that out loud. Humans don't know anything about that particular beverage. The wine is strong enough to affect paranormals. On a human it wouldn't take much before they were tanked.

"Sol?" I hear someone say my name and turn in time to see a male come over to me. He's someone I haven't seen in a long time. I stand and embrace Tristin in a hug. "I haven't seen you in forever," he says and leans back

"Tris! You look good. I didn't know you were working here."

He smiles. "Just helping out a friend. It's a short-time gig."

I've known him for probably three centuries. Our paths crossed one year in a tiny pub in Ireland. I was traveling, didn't have anywhere to go, so I went through Europe. Tris was tending bar and we spent all night talking. I ended up staying in town for a week to hang out with him. It was great having a friend, especially a fellow vampire.

"What are you doing down here?" he asks. I'm keenly aware of Lilah trying to busy herself near us. I have no doubt she's listening to our conversation.

"Ford and I own homes up in Duck now. I got bored last night and drove down here. Now I'm back for the…" I pick up the glass on the counter, "delicious water." I take a long swallow and let out an "Ahhhh." In truth, I hate being alone. Sure, I have my brother and friends, but I always feel like I'm an outsider trying to find my place. And now that everyone is finding their mates, I'm even more adrift.

Tris snorts. "Sure. The place is known for its… water." Then in my head he asks, *"You wouldn't be here because of the female behind the bar, would you?"*

*"You always were a smart paranormal."* I smile.

*"Be careful. She's tight with the owner. He told me to watch over her while I'm here."*

*"I'm not here to attack her. Geez, Tris."*

*"I didn't mean that. She's just not one to fool around with and*

*discard. I wasn't told her full story, but there's definitely one there."*

I lean back and peer at her over my shoulder. My eyes catch hers and she immediately looks away. *"I gathered that much last night when she tried to throw me out of here."*

He cocks his head. *"So, you're back anyway, even after being rejected?"* I shrug and he lets out a loud laugh. *"I never thought the famous Solomon Verascue would have to chase a female."*

*"Shut up."* I shove his shoulder, but he doesn't move thanks to his strength. I turn and face Lilah again. Tristin's laugh echoes around me as he goes to the kitchen to drop off an order. Lilah shakes her head.

"What?" I ask, certain I'm the reason she's doing so.

"How does everyone know you, yet I've never heard of you?"

"You must be very young. I'm quite worthy of gossip."

She ducks her head, which only confirms my suspicion that she is young. I wonder how old she truly is. Surely she's older than eighteen if she's working in a bar. Then again, paranormals don't go by traditional human age guidelines when we do things. I resist the pull to look inside her head.

With two large gulps, I down the rest of the water and place it back on the bar. "Can I have another water please, Lilah?"

She stiffens and glares at me. "I told you that's not my name."

"It is and I'm using it. If you don't like it, that's on you. I think it suits you."

"And I think the dent I'm going to make in your face is going to suit you."

"I love it when your claws come out, kitten."

She's about to say something back when Tris walks behind her and says something to her with his mind. She shakes her head and he quirks a brow. Her shoulders sag then she grabs my drink and fills it up. Tris winks at me. Such a mischievous vampire. One of the many reasons we get along. Lilah puts the glass back in front of me without another word.

Over the next two hours, I sit at the bar and people watch. I can't exactly stare at Lilah all night because that would border on creeper territory. While I may love the way she looks, I'm not some male who gets off by watching in a dark corner. Though I can't help but admire Lilah and the grace she has when working behind the bar. Every movement is like it's been practiced and honed. As if every step, every flick of her wrist, or drop of alcohol she pours, she's been doing for years upon years.

Right before closing time, and my fourth glass of water, mind you, a male stumbles through the door who clearly already had too many drinks. He's tall, balding, and has a big beer belly. His eyes are half-lidded and he barely lands on the stool two down from me. I was hoping he'd fall over and cause a scene. Pity. I could use some entertainment.

Lilah walks over to him. "We aren't serving you," she states firmly but nicely at the same time.

"Come on, sweetheart," he slurs. "I've got plenty of money." He pulls a wad of ones out of his pocket. Was he at a strip club before he came here? Who carries around that many singles?

Lilah pushes the money back toward him. "You've already had enough to drink. How about I call you a ride and let them take you home?"

"How about you take me home and ride me?"

I stand, ready to punch his face in. No one should say things like that to Lilah. She's moving before I can, gripping the front of his shirt, nearly tearing the fabric as she brings him close to where she leans over the bar. Her eyes flash sapphire and in turn, the male's eyes widen. But he's drunk enough that he'll play it off as a change in the lighting.

"If you don't get out of this bar, I'm going to remove you," she says low and deadly. It's a huge turn-on. Like, gigantic, how am I ever going to get this vision out of my head? It's an *I need her in the worst way* kind of thing.

He laughs then hiccups. "I'd like to see you try."

She reaches down with her free hand and plucks off one of her high heels. "You see this?"

He nods. "Yeah, they're sexy. How about you take everything off but them?" he slurs.

"How about I take this pointy, five-inch heel and ram it where the sun don't shine?" Could she get any hotter than she is at this moment?

The male's only response is to lick his lips and lean forward. That's enough of this.

I walk over to drunky and grip the back of his shirt, pulling him out of Lilah's grasp. He stumbles to his feet. I'm taller than him by a few inches. "If I were you, I'd go back to whatever hole you crawled out of and never step foot in this bar again."

"You can't tell me what to do!" he yells in my face. Sweet fate, what did he drink? Smells like turpentine mixed with vodka. My nose scrunches up as I turn my head to get away from his paint-peeling breath.

I maintain a tight hold as I drag him from the bar to the side of the building, where I teleport us next to the local police station and drop him down on the front steps. After a quick knock on the door, I walk back into the shadows and teleport back to the bar. The male needed to be taught a lesson. Not only is he now drunk on the steps of the police station, but I have no doubt he's going to start rambling off about how he has no idea how he got there, how some woman's eyes changed color, and how he suddenly appeared there without getting into a car. They're going to think he's high as a kite on top of being drunk. Hopefully, they'll put him in a cell overnight until he sobers up. I shudder at what would have happened if he tried to drive again. It's bad enough he drove to the bar.

"Where did you take him?" Lilah asks when I go back to my barstool.

"Away." I don't miss the other patrons at the bar eyeing me like I'm going to give them a juicy piece of gossip. When I offer nothing else, they turn back to their conversation.

"I was handling it," Lilah says low to me.

"And I handled it better." I shrug.

Her eyes narrow for a moment before she calls out, "Closing time! Drink up and go. You have five minutes." She turns to me. "That includes you."

I pick up my glass of water and take a sip. "I'm savoring this. Stop trying to ruin my delicious beverage. I need my palate cleansed after the breath of that loser."

She rolls her eyes and walks away, going about her business cleaning up behind the bar. Once the humans are gone, including the bartender and waitress, it's just Lilah, Tris, and me.

"You can go now," she tells me.

"I'm not leaving you alone. Who knows who else is out there?"

"You left me alone last night."

"That was different. I had to make an impression. Tonight, I'm here to make sure you're safe." The owner of the bar told Tris to watch over her for a reason. Now it's my mission to do so. At least here anyway. I'm not about to follow her to her home like a stalker unless she wants me there. Oh, how I'd love to be welcomed into her bed.

Lilah sighs and walks over to flip the lock on the front door.

"He's harmless," Tris says. "He's been my friend for many years. Honest, Conni."

"He's not harmless," she refutes. "He always has this twinkle in his eye that screams he's about to do something that's going to irritate me."

"Awww," I cut in. "You've noticed my eyes. If this isn't fate, I don't know what is." I lean toward her and bat my eyelashes. "Tell me what else you like about me. Is it my hair? The way my butt looks in these jeans?" I stand and turn, wiggling it at her.

"You're crazy!"

"So what if I am?" I stop my wiggling to face her. "Crazy is fun. Crazy is having a vampire shake his butt at you at two in the morning. There's nothing boring about me, kitten. And you're interested in my kind of insanity."

"You're lucky I don't let my cat out."

I smile. "There are so many things I can say in response to that. It's taking everything in me not to speak them all."

"You're ridiculous," she mutters before walking toward the back hallway. "Come on, Tristin, we have a bar to stock." He laughs and follows her.

I spend the time they're gone picking up the chairs and putting them on the tables. If I tried to help them restock, I'm sure I'd get yelled at. Out here I can clean up so she doesn't have to. If only I had a little fae magic to wash the floors.

Lilah and Tristin come back, each with a box of liquor in their arms, both carrying them with ease. Lilah sets hers on the counter and looks around at the now barren floor. With a quick twirl of her finger, all the crumbs, wrappers, every kind of filth is gone, and the floor is sparkling clean. Holy fate. She's not only a cat, but she's fae, too. This night just got a whole lot more interesting.

# CHAPTER SIX

*Lilah*

**TO SAY I SHOCKED** SOLOMON BY USING my magic last night is an understatement. He spent the next half hour following me around like a puppy, asking me a ton of questions I didn't answer. Finally, he let me get in my car and drive home. Sure, I could have opened a portal, but I like driving and I don't live far from the bar.

It took me a while to fall asleep. Every time I closed my eyes there was only one male there—Solomon. I hated it and loved it at the same time. Hated it because he really gets under my skin. Like deep in there to the point I want to get some cream and remove him like a rash. But the other part of me secretly loves the attention. Sure, he's pushy, but he doesn't try to grope me or do anything that would make me uncomfortable. He plays, teases, shows me this side of himself that's genuine. I've never met anyone like him.

I groan and roll to my side to look at the clock—ten in the morning. I wonder if Vanessa is up and around. I stand and rifle through my closet for something to wear. I could use my magic, but I learned early in life that not everyone takes kindly to someone who isn't pure fae or pure shifter.

Most are only one paranormal. I'm two. I've been made fun of, called names, bullied for years. I hated it. I've learned to hide my fae side. It's easier than hiding the shifter one.

Sometimes, no matter how much I try, I can't keep my cheetah at bay, and she always rises up to meet a challenge. As far as outward appearances, I look shifter, especially a cat. Tall, long legs, slender. My cat is made for speed. I don't have pointed ears or the luminescent skin most fae do, so there's no need for me to use glamour when I'm among humans.

After throwing on a pair of cutoff shorts, which I literally made from a pair of jeans when I moved to North Carolina, and a tank top, I sweep my hair into a high ponytail.

I was born and raised in Canada. My parents lived there. The mage who raised me lives there. Moving to the Outer Banks was a spur of the moment thing. I was here on a trip to try and get some sun—I had never seen the ocean before—and that's where I met Donovon. I didn't want to leave after that. The winters here are so much nicer compared to the frigid tundra up north. Now I call Nags Head home.

Time to open a portal. I raise my hands together and slowly arch them away to open one to Nessa's home. I always have it appear in my old bedroom because she leaves the door closed and never allows guests to sleep there. This way I get to pop in or out safely.

Stepping through, the cold of the portal washes over me, although as quickly as it's there, it's gone. I look around my old room and take in the warm quilt Ness made on the bed and the plants lined on the windowsill. I always loved them; my fae side calls out for nature. I'd use my magic to feed them and grow them. It was something I took pride in.

The closet door is still adorned with a rock band poster from years ago. Ness never took it down, nor did she change anything in the room. She said it will always be mine, and I'm the only one who can change it. I'm grateful to have her in my life.

Running my fingers over the oak footboard of the bed, I let out a wistful sigh before going to the door. I might not have come to Ness in the best way when I was little, but I don't for one second take for granted the love and kindness she gave me and still shows me. She's an amazing female.

I open the door and the scent of bacon immediately hits me as does Ness's humming. I sprint down the stairs, round the bottom of them, go down a short hallway, and stride into the kitchen where I find her in an apron with her back to me as she flips pancakes in one pan then bacon in the other.

"Morning, dear," she says without turning around. I bet she felt the magic of the portal when I opened it. Being a mage, she's very in tune with magic.

I walk over and kiss the top of her head. She's much shorter than me at five foot two; however, she makes up for it in her abilities. "Morning, Ness."

"Sit, I'll bring you breakfast." There are many days I still come here to eat, especially if I'm feeling out of place or off. This home and her presence always seem to ground me in a way nothing else ever has. She may not be my family by blood, although she is in my heart.

Ness turns around and I bust out laughing. She's wearing the apron I got her for Christmas as a prank. It has a white background with a woman's tanned beach body on the front, in a very skimpy bikini, with the head cut off. "I can't believe you're wearing that."

"Believe it. I had this on the other day and nothing

else." She winks.

"Let me guess. Roger was over."

"Of course he was." She shakes her curvy hips and smiles wide. "He can't resist what I have."

I laugh and put some pancakes and bacon onto my plate. "He has his hands full with you."

"You bet he does, especially when he's cupping my butt and—"

"Ness!" I shout. "Enough. I get it. I don't need a vivid picture of what you and your human do when I'm not here."

"Oh, please, Constance. You're nineteen years old. You know very well what adults do, especially when one of the adults is nine hundred and eighty. Honestly, child."

"There's a fine line between knowing and someone giving explicit details."

She shakes her head and piles her plate up with food. That's something else I love about her. We never lacked good food and great conversation. Ness has been the mother to me I needed.

"What's going on?" she asks.

I sigh. There's no trying to keep anything from her. I did when I first came to stay with her, but she broke down those barriers fast with her kind and loving nature. "There's this male—"

Her eyes widen. "And?"

"Let me get it out already. Geez." I roll my eyes. Ness wants me to find my mate as badly as Don does. She always tells me how she hates that I'm alone in Nags Head. But I'm not. I have Don and Jocelyn and Justin. "He came into the bar the other night, and then again last night. He drives me up the wall, but at the same time, I kind of like it. I'd never tell him that, though. He doesn't need me stroking his ego."

Vanessa smiles. "And who is this male? Maybe I know him."

"I'm sure you do. Everyone seems to but me. His name is Solomon Verascue." I prepare for her reaction. Ness is old enough that she should have heard of him. By what Don said, almost everyone has.

A slow smile spreads across her face. "You could do much worse than a Verascue. They have one of the purest bloodlines out there."

"He's not a thoroughbred, Ness. He's a vampire."

"A very strong vampire, with a family who can wipe the floor with almost every paranormal on the planet. I once saw Solomon's mother, Eloise, pick up a bear shifter by his nether regions and launch him across the forest. The sound that shifter made will haunt me forever. This high-pitched shriek followed by a thud as he slammed into a tree." She shakes herself as if to rid her mind of the memory.

"What did the shifter do to her to cause that kind of reaction?"

"Hit on her. And by hit on her, I mean he put his arm around her and licked the shell of her ear. He was brazen. Apparently, he wasn't aware of who she was, or that she was mated to Seth since the beginning of time. You don't mess with the Verascues."

"I'm not messing with anyone at the moment. He's the one pursuing me, not the other way around."

"You're lucky," she says, pointing her fork at me before stabbing another piece of pancake.

"I don't feel lucky. I feel exposed and raw when he's around. He can break down the block you put on my mind. He knows my real name, however, he said he didn't dig deeper."

"Of course he can break it down. The raw power running through that family isn't like anything I've ever seen. If nothing else, make a friend out of him and keep him as an ally."

"You sound like Don," I mutter.

"Now he's a smart bear. Never gave anyone a reason to grip him down below and toss him through the air."

"That we know of." I have no doubt Don has a deeply buried wild side. One that was in full force before he bought the bar and gutted it, making it into what it is today.

"What's holding you back?" she asks. "That male is attractive. I've seen him in passing, though we never formally met."

"I don't want to be in a relationship. I don't want a mate. I like being on my own with no one to answer to. And Solomon, I get the feeling he's a player. If I'm ever going to contemplate seeing if I'm fated to someone, it will be with a person who'll be mine and only mine. Not someone who could grow bored of me and leave when I least expect it."

Ness reaches over, places her hand on mine, and gently squeezes it. "We don't get to choose our mates. If Solomon is it, then so be it. Besides, he might be a player now, but once he finds the one fated for him, I'll put all of my money on him settling down faster than you can blink. A mate who would never leave your side."

I don't have the best role models for relationships. My father left me with Vanessa when I was a small child. He couldn't handle the fae side of me. Said it reminded him too much of my mother. So the only real paranormal I look up to is Nessa. She's been steadfast in her love for me, but she hasn't found her mate. I only see her, not a relationship between two paranormals. No undying love. No lasting bond. I know firsthand how cruel the world can be. Love doesn't always conquer all.

Instead of replying, I continue to eat while she watches me. I'm sure she's picturing me mated.

Maybe I could be friends with Solomon. Maybe I'll want to shove him through a wall because he doesn't know when to shut his mouth. Or maybe I'll be pleasantly surprised and he turns out to be a nice male. There's only one way to find out. If I don't try, I'll always be wondering what if. It's bad enough he's taking up so much of my headspace. At least if I prove he's a jerk, I can push him out of there once and for all. That doesn't mean this will be easy for me.

With the food settling in my stomach like a boulder, I push the plate aside and try to figure out how to even approach any kind of friendship with the vampire who makes me see red because of his attitude. Everyone thinks it's a good idea. Tristin surely gets along with him. Not that I know Tristin well, but if he's a friend of Don's, then he's a good male in my book. Besides, Solomon wouldn't have a reputation for being a good male if he were horrible. And Don and Ness wouldn't push me toward having a relationship with him if he were. I just hope I don't end up choking on those words later when his attitude and cockiness turn out to be who he really is and my thoughts of him being more go up in smoke.

Glancing up, I notice Ness smiling at me. "Smart girl," she says. I must have given my decision away with my expression.

"Shut up," I grumble, causing her to laugh.

"I do love you, my dear."

"Love you, too, Ness."

# CHAPTER SEVEN

## *Solomon*

**"WOULD YOU STOP** PACING?" FORD YELLS. "You're making me insane."

"It's not a far trip, brother," I reply wryly.

"Go to the bar. See your female. I don't get why this is so difficult for you."

"Well, for one, she's not my female. And two, I don't know how to do this! I'm a love 'em and leave 'em type of male. I don't do friendships or feelings. This is all foreign to me."

"Times are changing, Sol. There's something about this female that draws you in. Stop fighting it."

It's been four days since I've seen Lilah. I'm going out of my mind. I thought maybe if I put some distance between us, my feelings would calm down, but just the opposite happened. With every night I don't see her, my skin starts to itch more and more. It's getting out of hand. Screw it. It's already out of hand.

I'm not sure what's going on. She's all I think about. I can't get her out of my head.

I stop pacing and face Ford. "Come with me." He's got

his feet kicked up on the coffee table and he's lounging back on the couch. "Sienna's with Ari babysitting the twins. You have hours before she'll be back. You know how Wake and Paige get on their date nights. They forget what time it is and don't come crawling home until early in the morning." And rightfully so. Having two girls that are the same age at once has to be a lot to handle. I'm surprised they don't go on dates more often for sanity's sake.

Ford watches me, his expression never changing. Still the contemplative one. "You need me to go, don't you? You've never needed my help with a female in the past and I highly doubt you need it now. You're insecure over this one. It's odd."

"By all means, just point out every one of my flaws."

He chuckles. "I didn't mean it in a bad way. Just that this is new for you and you're not sure what to do with it."

"Ya think?" I retort loudly.

He drops his feet to the ground and leans forward with his elbows on his knees. "I'll go on one condition." I teleport to my house, grab my car fob, and teleport back before tossing it at him. He's loved my car since I bought it. He could buy one, but I think he likes bothering me all the time so he can take it for a spin with Sienna.

He grips the fob tightly. "Okay, let's go. Let me meet this female and see if she's worthy of my brother." I let out a sigh of relief. Hopefully, Ford will be able to tell me if I'm losing my mind. Or if there's something there between Lilah and me.

We teleport into my garage and open the door to let the salty, incredibly warm air in. Ford and I get into the car and, once it's started, he immediately cranks up the air-conditioning, which I'm grateful for. I don't really want windblown hair tonight and neither does Ford.

Traffic isn't too bad this time of night. The tourist crowd is settled in their rental homes for the evening. The people out now are the ones who like the bar scene and don't need to get up early in the morning. Ford pulls into the bar's parking lot and kills the engine.

"Have you met the owner yet?" he asks.

"No, but he's a bear shifter."

"Gee, what gave it away?" He deadpans and points to the wooden sign with the bar's logo on it.

I shove his shoulder. "Shut up."

We get out of the car and I take notice of a packed parking lot. Music is coming from inside, getting louder when someone opens the door to leave. Ford holds the door for me. Inside, it looks like a different place. There's a band playing in the back. No stage but an area cleared away of tables to make room for them. All the remaining tables are filled, so is each barstool, and there are people leaning against the walls with drinks in hand, listening to the music.

"You didn't tell me how popular this place was," Ford says near my ear.

"It hasn't been like this the other times I was here."

I grip his arm and nod toward the bar so we can make our way over. Lilah and Justin, I think that's his name, are slinging drinks left and right, filling orders. She's as stunning as ever in a Grizzly Don's tank top and short black shorts.

*"That's your female?"* Ford asks in my mind.

*"Not mine, but yes."*

*"She's very attractive, Sol. I can see what drew you to her."*

I turn and glare hard at him; my fangs descend upon their own accord.

He puts his hands up. *"Easy, brother. I have no interest in her. I have no interest in any female outside of my mate. Take it down a notch."* He's right. I shake my head, not understanding the reaction I just had. Ford's my brother. He'd never go after what's mine, especially now that he has Sienna. Not that Lilah is mine or anything.

Lilah turns and brings a drink over to the male beside Ford then looks up and stops short. "Fresh hell, there's two of you."

I smile wide and sling my arm over Ford's shoulders. "Allow me to introduce you to Ford. He's my much younger and less charming brother."

He elbows me in the side. "I'm his better looking, stronger, and smarter brother." Ford holds out his hand for Lilah. "Ford Verascue. Nice to meet you."

Lilah looks down for a moment, seeming to consider the offer, then takes his hand in hers. "Constance Levise. Nice to meet you as well."

"Hey," I speak up. "How come you shook his hand but never shook mine? I'm hurt."

She rolls her eyes, completely ignoring my question. "What can I get you, or are we going with water and a side of seeing how far you can push me tonight?"

"Water, but with a side of lime if you must know," I reply in a faux haughty voice. Her lips quirk up on one side and internally I do a cheer that I almost got a smile out of her.

"And for you?" she asks Ford.

"Water and a burger. I'm hungry."

"Sienna didn't let you feed before she left?" I ask quietly but Ford will hear me. Glancing up, I notice Lilah watching and no doubt listening to us.

"She did but I want a burger. I haven't had one in a while."

"Two waters and a burger coming up," Lilah states and turns to give the cook Ford's order.

Ford turns toward me. "I thought you told me her name was Lilah. She introduced herself as Constance."

"Her name is Lilah Constance, but she doesn't like her first name for some reason. I could find out, however, I don't want to dig around her head. I like her name and every time I say it, it has the bonus of irritating her, so I use it whenever I can." I smile wide.

I notice a flash of white hair coming our way. Tristin breaks through the crowd with a tray tucked under his arm. "Sol! It's so good to see you. I wondered if something happened since you hadn't been back. I thought for sure Conni got her claws into you and finally drove you away."

"Oh, she has her claws buried deep in him," Ford states with mirth.

Tris turns to him. "Ford! I didn't know he'd bring you." Tris leans in and embraces my brother. "Hey, what are you doing tonight after the bar closes? I'd love to catch up." I automatically glance over to Lilah, where she's filling two glasses with water. Her eyes lift and catch mine, but she quickly returns to her task.

"Well, Sol is no doubt going to hang here, but I'm free," Ford replies. "We can see what kind of trouble we can get into."

"Sounds good." Tris smiles. A bell dings from the back, alerting him to a completed food order. "I've gotta go, but don't leave without me."

"No worries. I'll be here," Ford replies.

Tris is off to the kitchen as the band plays the final notes of their song. The crowd applauds and they announce they're taking a break. People clap them on the shoulders as they pass by, telling them how much they love their music.

Lilah walks back over, immediately drawing my attention to her as if nothing else in here exists. She places the glasses down on coasters then wipes her forehead with the back of her hand. A drop of sweat trickles down from her temple to her cheek and I'm absolutely mesmerized by it. I want to lick it from her skin. Groaning, I force myself to look away.

Nothing is going as it should. When I first came to this bar, it was to find a female to take home, and not only did I find that, but I discovered someone I never saw coming. I can picture her staying in my bed: sleeping, loving, living. My body goes rigid. Nope. Not going there. She's just a female I find attractive, nothing more.

*"Keep telling yourself that, brother,"* Ford states with a chuckle in my mind.

*"Get out of my head."* I glare at him and throw up a block he can't break through. With Lilah in front of me, I let my guard down. I wonder what Tris heard.

*"Everything!"* Tris shouts in my mind. For fate's sake! I must have let that thought slip through. I sit up straight and peer over the crowd until I find Tris smiling at me. I flip him off and return my attention to the glass in front of me. Hopefully, Lilah didn't hear anything. I don't think I dropped my guard that much. Tris is powerful.

At least Ford has met her now and can tell me what he thinks later. Not that I expect him to learn much in the short time we've been here. Plus, I wouldn't blame him if he hated her. After all, I hated Sienna for a long time. It took a lot for me to finally come around and embrace her relationship with my brother. But at the end of the day, Ford's happiness means the world to me, and I'll do whatever it takes so he never feels an ounce of pain again. I'll always be there to look out for him and help protect him and his mate.

"Well, this is dreadful," a female voice says behind me,

causing me to jump slightly on the barstool. Lovely. Just what my night needed.

"Mother," Ford says coolly. "What do we owe the privilege of your visit? And please tell me you used the door like an average person." I don't miss Ford saying person instead of human.

"Honestly, Ford. Did you think I was going to snap my fingers and suddenly appear in front of so many, exposing us for what we really are? You act like I'm twenty-five."

"No, I'm acting like you're completely unpredictable. I never know what you're going to do or say next."

She pats him on the shoulder then turns her attention to me. I meet Ford's eyes and hope to convey an SOS message to help get me out of this situation because I have no doubt why she's here.

"Of course you know," she says. "You'd be a fool not to. Now, point me in the direction of your female."

Lilah comes up as the word female leaves my mom's lips. "I'm not his female," she says, but with no fire in her voice.

My mom looks her up and down. "I'm not so sure about you."

Lilah crosses her arms. "And I'm not so sure about you. You don't get to come in here and start judging me."

"No, I did that the moment I knew my son had an interest in you. I also knew all I needed to before coming here. But sometimes it's better to see things with your own eyes rather than judge from afar."

Lilah looks at me. "I don't think you're too bad compared to her." She juts her chin toward my mom.

I smile. "I'll take that as a compliment." Mom smacks me up the back of my head. "Ow! What did you do that for?"

"I'm your mother." That's all the explanation I get. Not that I expected more.

"Now, Lilah, tell me about yourself."

"If you haven't noticed, I'm a bit busy."

Mom waves her hand dismissively. "They can wait."

"Wow, just when I think Solomon is cocky, I meet you."

Mom rolls her eyes. "Not cocky, dear. Confident."

# CHAPTER EIGHT

*Lilah*

**IT ALL MAKES SENSE NOW.** WHY SOLOMON behaves as he does. It has everything to do with his mother. She's ten times worse than him in terms of being full of themselves. I just have to keep chanting in my head to be nice and make friends. If Don knew Eloise was in his bar and I treated her awfully, he'd throw a fit.

I choke back an insult and ask, "Would you like something to drink?"

She smiles and looks like the predator she is. "No, but thank you for asking. That must have been hard for you." To my surprise, I start to smile.

"Oh, no," Ford says quietly to Solomon, although not really since I can easily hear him. "They're bonding."

Eloise turns toward him. "And where is your female?"

"Babysitting."

"She should be home with you trying to make me some grandchildren."

Ford stands. "That's it. I'm out. I love you, brother, but I didn't sign on to deal with our mother tonight."

Solomon gapes at him. "You can't leave me."

"I can and I will." He turns toward Eloise. "I'd say it's a pleasure, but that's a lie. Maybe next time you visit, you lay off the grandchildren talk and try making normal conversation."

She smiles at him, no doubt speaking to him with her mind because a moment later he's smiling back. They both might be a lot of talk, but I can tell they love one another.

Ford peers over his shoulder and catches Tris's eyes. Tris nods then Ford is making his way out the door. I heard them making plans before.

When I look back at Solomon, I find him watching me, not paying any attention to his mother. I turn and stalk away, not liking for one second being under his penetrating glare. I don't return to him until Ford's burger is done but since he's no longer here, I set it down between Solomon and Eloise. What shocks me to my core is when Eloise picks it up and eats it like everyone else in the bar would. The difference is that she has this air of sophistication. She's dressed very well and has a diamond necklace on. Her hair is perfectly styled in soft waves. Not a flyaway hair in sight. It's fascinating watching her eat the burger with her pink manicured nails and then lick ketchup off them.

She glances up at me. "Did you need something?" Any other paranormal would probably scurry away, but I've never been called normal.

"I find this whole thing interesting. To me, you'd appear more at home somewhere that served very tiny portions at a high price."

Instead of replying out loud, she does so in my head. *"I'm four thousand years old, Lilah."* I bristle and open my mouth to correct my name. This is the second time she's said it. She stops me by speaking again. *"That's your name and the one I'll use. I'm not about to call you by your middle name. You should be proud of the name you were given. I don't care that the man who fathered you gave it to you. Own that name. By not acknowledging it, he wins. He should never win regarding you."*

I nod. *"I understand your reasoning, however, I can't just turn my feelings off. Obviously, you've taken the grand tour of my head and realize what a horrible shifter he is."*

*"I'm not telling you not to feel. I'm telling you not to hide. And yes, of course I looked into your mind and memories. My son has an interest in you, and I had to make sure you were a solid female. That you're worthy of him."*

*"Am I?"* I'm not sure why I ask. I don't need her approval. I also don't need to have anything to do with her son. But there's something about her that makes me want to live to a higher standard. Like she's pushing me without doing anything. Maybe that push isn't a bad thing.

*"I think so, but only time will tell. You're very young, but you've had a hard life. You don't trust easily, which is actually a good thing since there are too many awful paranormals out there who would take advantage of you.*

*"You conceal your magic well, though I think you should show it more. Yes, there are some out there who will have an opinion and voice how it isn't right that species mix, but they are nothing to you. If, and I am saying if, anything does happen between you and my son, you'll never need to hide because you'll have our backing. And I would never ask you to.*

*"You have the best of two worlds inside of you. You have the speed and strength of a shifter. Your cheetah has keen instincts and skills. Your fae side possesses magic, which, let's face it, can come in very handy. Those two combined, plus a few vampire bites to give you more powers, no one would ever mess with you again."*

I shift from one foot to the other under her scrutinizing gaze. I understand what she's saying and her reasoning, but just like using my first name, it won't come easy to change. I've been hiding my fae side for a long time, only letting it show in front of a select few.

Solomon plucks the burger from the plate in front of his mother.

"No one told you that you could eat that," she says with a hint of anger in her tone.

"And no one told you to sit here and have a conversation with Lilah I can't hear. Although, I could have if I wanted to, but I thought I'd give you two some privacy since it's obvious you had something to work out. Are you done now? I'm bored of watching people play darts while the band is still on a break."

"For fate's sake, Solomon, you're not a child who needs to be entertained at all times," Eloise chides. "You're a grown male who can occupy himself."

"Yes, well, the female's time I want to occupy is currently talking to my mother," he hisses.

"As fun as all this is," I interrupt. "I have other people to tend to." With that, I turn and make my way down the bar, filling drinks, giving refills to those at the tables.

The band finally goes back to their spot and begins to play. Before I realize it, hours have gone by and it's closing time. My body doesn't ache thanks to my fae side, which always heals. Although, it doesn't erase my exhaustion. I need sleep.

I don't even realize Solomon is still sitting at the bar when I walk back from locking the front door. He's talking to Tristin and I don't bother to interrupt them. I simply go and grab more liquor to restock so we're ready for tomorrow. Nights when a band plays really depletes some of our stock, but it's for the best. This place is amazing, and I love seeing it filled to the brim. Too bad Don is still away, or he could be here paying attention to Solomon and no doubt finding out about his interests pertaining to me.

When I finish stocking the bar, Tristin says goodnight and teleports away with a smile. Oh, sure. Leave me alone with the other vampire. Just what I need. That's not dangerous at all.

"You don't need to stay. I'm quite capable of getting to my car," I tell Solomon.

"I know, but I want to spend time with you." I stop at his words. I didn't expect him to say something so honest and real. I expected another smart comment.

"Why?" I ask. Then I remember the last time I asked why tonight to Eloise, I got an explanation I wasn't ready for. I need to learn to be quiet and stop asking so many freaking questions.

Solomon stands and slowly walks over to me. It's then I take him in. Not his clothes, but the way he walks. My eyes are immediately drawn to his waist and the way his hips move with each step. He's not overly thin, but slender. I have no doubt there are a host of muscles under his shirt. He's walking sin. I shouldn't want him. I shouldn't find him attractive, but how can I not? He's the perfect male specimen.

As my gaze wanders from his hips to his stomach and chest, up his neck to his jaw and lips, I finally stop when I reach his eyes. There is so much heat in them; I'm surprised I don't burn up on the spot. Solomon is an older and experienced vampire with a pure bloodline. He could definitely take anything I dish out. The question is, do I want to dish it out? To him?

He stops mere inches from me—his grey eyes sparkle in the light of the empty bar. His blond hair is combed back from his face and my fingers itch to thread into it to find out if it's as soft as it looks. I don't dare touch him, though.

I'm too afraid to. What if I do and find out he's my mate? I don't want that. I don't want to need another paranormal. I don't want what happened to my parents to happen to me. What if I find the one I love and they die? Or what if they walk away from me? I couldn't handle losing the other half of my soul. I watched what it did to my father.

I take a measurable step back. "I can't."

He cocks his head slightly to the side. "You can't what? I didn't say anything. I didn't ask you a question. I didn't even reach out to touch you. All I did was walk toward you."

"There can never be anything between us, Solomon."

"Sol. You don't need to be formal."

"Whatever. The point still stands. I don't want a mate. I don't need a male in my life. I'm happy on my own."

"Are you?"

I shrug. "Even if I weren't, it doesn't matter to you. I control my own happiness." I learned long ago not to depend on anyone else to be happy.

He steps closer. I retreat. We do this dance until I'm backed into the far wall with nowhere left to go.

"I'm not going to hurt you," he says quietly.

"Not physically." I swallow at his intense gaze.

"Why do you think I'd hurt you emotionally?"

I don't answer but instead use a little burst of magic to push him back a foot so I can get away from him. I should have thought to do that before.

"Lilah, would you stop? Please?" The pleading tone in his voice almost has me doing just that, but instead, I go behind the bar, count out the register and close things down, then grab my keys. I can't stay in here anymore with him. I can already feel my resolve crumbling and that's not a good thing.

Walking over to the front door, I stop when I reach it and flip the lock. Going through the bar to the back door would give us more privacy. Out front, people drive by. I don't want to be alone with Solomon any longer. I need to get away. I open the door and wait for him to step beside me.

"After you," he says and sweeps out his arm. I resist rolling my eyes. I'm trying too hard not to lean in and smell him. I've caught hints of his scent before. It's like he bottled the ocean and sun and somehow made it into a cologne. But I bet it's even better up close with my nose grazing the skin of his neck.

I internally shake the thought away and step outside then turn and lock the door once he's through. The second I make a move toward my car, Solomon grips my waist and pulls me to his side. Luckily, it's only our clothes that touch. No skin.

*"Don't move,"* he says in my head in a hard tone. Alarm bells immediately sound in my mind. Something's wrong. His body is rigid against mine as I scan our surroundings, not sure what's going on.

That's when I hear it—a faint crackle. It turns into a slow hiss. Solomon lifts his hand to snap and teleport us away, but he's too slow. There's a loud bang and we're both thrown into the middle of the road, along with dust and debris. We land hard on our sides. The screech of tires causes my eyes to open so I can witness an SUV narrowly miss us.

# CHAPTER NINE

## *Solomon*

**RINGING IN MY EARS** CAUSES EVERYTHING ELSE to be muffled as I open my eyes and try to catch my bearings. My body heals quickly, the ringing slowly fading as my gaze catches on the female next to me and the blood running from the side of her head.

Panic rushes through me with a force I've never felt before as I reach out and pull her close. Cars stop near us, but before anyone can get out, I snap and teleport us to my home in Duck. I don't care if they saw. It was dark. At least there was that. I have to make sure Lilah is okay, though. She's all that matters.

Carefully, I stand in my living room, bringing her with me, and place her on the couch. Her eyes flutter open, finally regaining consciousness.

"What happened?" she mutters.

"I'm not sure. One second we were beside the bar and the next we were in the road."

"There was an explosion." She tries to sit up quickly, but I hover over her, not wanting her to move yet.

"Don't get up. You need to shift to heal."

She pushes against me. I don't miss how she's careful not to let our skin touch. How easy it would be to reach out and caress her skin to see what her reaction would be. "I don't. I'm half fae. I'm already healed." Oh, right. I knew that.

"Are you okay?" I ask.

"Do you think I'm okay?" she yells. "Someone just blew up the bar and we were nearly roadkill."

I scoff. "A car running us over wouldn't have killed us. It would have hurt, but we wouldn't be dead."

"I'm so glad you can find humor in a time like this," she deadpans and fully shoves me away so she can stand. She takes a moment to look around. "Where are we?"

"My home."

Even in the darkened room I don't miss the quirk of her eyebrow. Oh, how I love night vision. "Desperate times, huh?" I do enjoy her sassy mouth.

"Please. If I wanted to get you to come home with me, I could have done it by now. This wasn't some ploy. It was the first place I thought of when I was trying to get us out of the middle of the street before we had tire tread stamped on our faces."

"So the parking lot of the bar wasn't an option? It was feet away."

I walk over to stand in front of her, anger coursing through me. "And then what? Put you in a vulnerable position with whomever just blew that place up? I don't think so."

She curses under her breath and pulls her phone out of her pocket. The screen is cracked, but it still works as she taps on it a few times and puts it to her ear. The phone rings on the other end.

"Hello," comes a male voice, groggy with sleep.

"Don, I have to tell you something."

"Constance? What happened? Are you okay?" His words are rushed, concern evident in his tone. Maybe he's not a horrible male if his first thought is of her and not the bar. I have no doubt this is the shifter who owns it.

"There was an explosion."

"What? At the bar?" he roars. "Open a portal right now and come to me. I need to see that you're okay."

She sighs. "I can't open a portal since I have no idea where you are. I've never been there."

Not caring if she yells at me, I pluck the phone from her hand and speak to the male on the other end. "Where are you? I'll teleport to you."

"Tristin?"

"No, Solomon Verascue," I say in an even tone. Usually I'd use this opportunity to embrace my cockiness and throw my family name around, but there's no time for that now.

"Oh, um, this is Donovan Rossmisin. I'm the owner of the bar."

"I've gathered that much. Tell me where you are and I'll teleport us as close as I can, then we'll walk until we get to you. I can teleport you to the bar so you can survey the damage." He quickly tells me his approximate location, which is clear on the other side of the country in the mountains surrounding Lake Tahoe. I hang up and face Lilah.

"You're not leaving me here," she says.

"I never said I was." I hold out my bare hand and she shakes her head. Stubborn female. I clasp her around the waist and snap.

It's pitch-black where we land and we begin walking

toward the peak of the mountain as directed. It's quiet with only the sounds of nature around us. Our steps are almost soundless.

Trees rustle. Branches snap. There's something or someone coming toward us. I'm almost positive it's the bear shifter, but until I'm certain, I'll protect the female by my side with everything I have.

Seconds later, a massive grizzly bear breaks through the trees, stopping mere feet from us. My fangs descend, ready to go against it. But in my next breath, he shifts.

Donovon is no small bear shifter in human form. He's tall and wide with plenty of muscles. His brown hair is pushed back from his face as if he'd run his fingers through it over and over. He wastes no time rushing forward to hug Lilah.

Pure jealousy flows through me. It's completely foreign, but I don't give myself time to analyze it at the moment. Instead, I embrace it as my hands fist by my sides and my fangs remain out. It's taking everything in me to hold myself back from ripping the two of them apart.

Luckily, Donovon pulls away from her. When his gaze lands on me, he immediately steps back two paces with his hands up. I look to Lilah and see her lips part as her eyes settle on my fangs. There's no missing the heat in those eyes. So, the female does like my jealousy. Interesting.

"I mean no harm," Donovan says gently.

Unclenching my fists, I force myself to calm down and let my fangs retract. I turn to give him my full attention. "Yeah, well, you'll have to excuse me after the night we've had. I'm a little on edge." I'm not apologizing, but I'm also not admitting to what just happened. Although, any idiot could see how defensive I became when the male touched Lilah.

"Can you take me there?" Donovon asks.

I nod. "I can and I will, but we don't want to rush in there without a plan. There will no doubt be a lot of cops surrounding the place. We have to get our stories straight. You can say you were visiting family and were on your way to the bar when Lilah called you. Instead of going right there, you went to her to make sure she was safe. This is just for the story. Because they will ask where she and I were. Whoever did this could be there but hiding, waiting to see what their handiwork did, or they fled after it happened. Either way, we have to be on the lookout for anyone suspicious. Also, if anything gets too heated, or the cops start looking at any of us suspiciously, I'll scrub their minds and give them the story I just told you." I take a breath and turn toward Lilah.

"As for you and me," I start. "We walked out of the bar, you locked up, and then there was an explosion. I helped you to the nearby house where I made sure you were okay before returning. You're scared and shaken. You have to work that angle to make it believable. Or else they'll think you fled the scene out of guilt. I wonder how many saw us lying in the middle of the road and suddenly disappear."

"You teleported in front of humans?" Donovon asks incredulously.

I shrug, not caring. "I had to get us out of there fast and Lilah was knocked out. I wasn't about to carry her to the bar and hand her over to whatever person did this."

"Paranormal," Donovon corrects.

"You know that with certainty? Because I don't. Who's to say it was a paranormal or a human? In all honesty, I'm leaning toward human. A paranormal would be more creative, or so I'd like to think. Then again, not everyone can be as brilliant as me."

"Even in a time like this, you manage to find a way to compliment yourself," Lilah observes.

I smile. "I am rather talented." She rolls her eyes in response.

"Can we get this done so I can see if there is any of my bar still standing?" Donovon asks.

"Right." I hold out my hand for his and wait for Lilah to walk over. To my astonishment, she sidles up next to her friend and puts her arm around his waist in a move that screams comfort and love. Donovon does the same to hold her close. My jaw immediately clenches.

"We're not mates," Donovon says quietly and slowly, as if I'm a second away from ripping out his throat. Well, I'm not a second away. More like a minute.

Lilah smacks him on the arm with the other hand. "That's none of his business."

"I'm afraid you're wrong there, Conni," he replies. "It appears it's completely his business."

"What are you getting at?" she asks and tries to pull her arm away, but he doesn't let her, only tightens his grip.

"Later. Right now, I want to get to the bar."

I'm not sure what's going on here, but Donovon is right. Now isn't the time to try and analyze whatever's happening here. We have to handle things back in Nags Head first.

With a quick snap of my fingers, I bring us outside a house two doors down from the bar, under the raised deck where it's dark and we're easily hidden.

We let go of one another and begin to make the short walk to the bar. We're sure to stick to the shadows where no one will see us until we're ready to be revealed.

"Holy fate," Donovon whispers as we reach the building.

The entire side of the bar is blown off from the back entrance to the front. There's one wall that remains standing. I can clearly see inside to where the bar was. Nothing but debris remains. Firemen surround the place as they try to put out the last of the flames while multiple police officers speak with people nearby, who I have no doubt are residents or tourists staying close to the bar.

"Where were you?" a male shouts from behind us, causing us to jump and spin around simultaneously. Luckily, with all the commotion at the bar, the first responders didn't hear him—Tristin. "I was worried sick! Ford's mate asked him to go to the Avynwood Pack House, so I was left on my own for the night. I heard the explosion from the place I'm renting and teleported back, but there was no one here. Except your car, Conni. So I thought for sure you were buried under the rubble somewhere." I look Tris up and down and take in his singed shirt and sooty legs. He must have run into the building looking for her. I always knew he was a good male.

"I'm sorry," Lilah says. "We ended up in the middle of the road and Solomon teleported us away then we went to get Don."

It's then Tris realizes there's someone else with us. He rushes forward and embraces the shifter in a tight hug. "This wasn't how I thought our reunion would go." He smiles.

"So good to see you," Don replies. "Have you spoken to the cops?"

Tris shakes his head. "No. Once I didn't find anyone in there, I teleported here, out of sight."

Donovon takes a long look at his bar. His shoulders slouch. This male obviously loved this place. It has to be hard seeing everything you worked for destroyed to a pile of wood.

"I'll help you rebuild," I immediately offer. I'm not sure where it came from since I've never been one for manual labor. Tearing throats out of paranormals, sure. Building anything, not a chance.

All three paranormals swing their gazes to mine in utter shock.

"What? I can do stuff." Tris looks at me questionably. "Fine." I sigh. "I can pay people to do stuff."

"And now we're back to the Sol I know and love."

"Oh, shut up," I say and bump my shoulder against his. "I have very capable hands that I use when I need to."

Chuckling, Tris replies, "I remember when we found these two males outside the bar back home and they were harassing a female. You didn't hesitate to dismember one of them. Right in front of her." Lilah gasps.

I rush to clear the air because this paints me in a very bad light. "In all fairness, I read his mind before I did it and saw the things he'd done. He should have been killed a long time before I found him." Something in Lilah's gaze changes, but it's only for a second and then it's gone. At least she doesn't seem appalled anymore. That male was a rapist. The things he'd done… I still get angry when I think about it.

# CHAPTER TEN

## *Lilah*

**"NO, ABSOLUTELY NOT,"** I SAY WITH CONVICTION.

"You can't go with Tris, and I'm not going to be around for a bit," Don states. "This is the best option."

"For whom? Because as I see it, it's for everyone but me." I cross my arms and stare at the three males in front of me. Don, Solomon, and Tristin are all standing shoulder to shoulder like a wall of alphas. And all of their gazes are on me.

"Geez, you act like I'm going to tie you to the bed and never let you up. Unless you're into that kind of thing," Sol states with mirth.

"See!" I yell. "This is what I'm going to have to deal with!"

We're standing in the living room of my small apartment above the garage owned by a little old lady. The garage is a free-standing structure, separate from the house. I've lived here since I met Don, or around there. But right now, the males want me to leave the space I've called home. All because they have no clue who blew up the bar and they want me safe. I get that. But the thing is, I don't want to live with Sol. I want to stay here. I can take care of myself.

"You can," Sol states, reading my mind. "No one is questioning that. But there is still someone out there, and we don't know if he's after you or Don or Tris."

"So I'm supposed to stay with you when whoever this is could be after you? How is that going to keep me safe? To me it sounds like I'll be put in harm's way."

"I've told you," Don cuts in, his tone placating. "Solomon and his family are very powerful. Anyone would be a fool to go up against them."

"And I didn't say we'll be staying in Duck," Sol adds. "I have homes all over the world. We could go anywhere."

"Yeah, so can I," I interject. "I can open a portal. Remember?"

"Would you feel safer in the fae realm?" he asks.

"No, not at all." I've never actually been there, and as much as I don't want to stay with Sol, the idea of going to another realm causes anxiety to flood through me at a rapid pace. My palms start to sweat and my heart begins to race.

"I know one of the princes. He's a great paranormal. Actually, my whole family is tight with the royals. You'd be well protected there." Of course, he's friends with the fae royal family. Sol is, in no formal terms, a prince among vampires.

"I said no," I all but growl.

"Conni," Don says carefully, using the voice that can knock down my defenses. "I have to get back to my family. I need to know you're safe so I can deal with the matter there." And there's the guilt trip. Though, I'm not sure how much of a guilt trip it is if his words are true. Don does need to get back. I'd hate to think of him not being there for the death of his father because he was babysitting me. Or unable to enjoy the last bit of time he has left with the male.

He's playing dirty.

"Fine," I relent and Sol beams. Jerk vampire. "I have a few conditions, though."

"Name them," Sol says.

"One, I want my own room. Two, you can't enter the room unless you have my permission and that includes teleporting in."

"What if you're in danger?"

"I thought you said I'd be safe with you." Don glares at me. "Fine. Only if there is imminent danger. Three, I'm not to be treated like a prisoner. I'm free to come and go as I please."

"As long as I'm with you," Sol adds.

"This should do wonders for my dating life." Don opens his mouth, about to cut in and no doubt say how I have zero dating life, but I glare at him until he closes his mouth.

"If you think I'm going to let you turn my home into a casual place to hook up, you're way off the mark," Sol replies in a harsh tone. I look over at him and don't miss the fire in his eyes. There's that jealous side of him again. I like it. Way too much. It does something inside of me. Lights a fire that was never lit before.

"I have some rules of my own," Sol begins. "No leaving without me. We just covered this, but I'm reiterating it. No bringing your car. We're not sure if whoever did this is tracking you and they're aware of what you drive. I can teleport and you can open a portal. We don't need a car. And finally, this is the most important one, if something happens, or I suspect it's about to, I need to know you'll listen to me and not question my motives. I've walked this world for a long time. I've seen things most would think could only be found in nightmares. I trust my instincts above everything else and they're the reason I'm still alive." I nod because if something does happen, he'll keep me safe. He proved that already when the bar blew up.

All the males stare at me, waiting for what I'll say next. But at this point, it's either stand here and stare back or go pack. Packing wins.

Spinning on my heel, I turn for my bedroom and pull out my tattered old suitcase. My father had tossed it at me when I was a young child and told me to put my belongings in it. That I wasn't coming back, so take everything I wanted. What did I know? I was only four. But I packed what was important to me at the time: stuffed animals, pretty dresses my mom had bought me, and the only picture I had left of her. The other photos we had around the house my dad had torn up then burned.

I have no doubt he loved my mom. None. He was a loyal mate to her. However, that changed when she died giving birth to me. He tried to raise me. Tried to be who I needed. That was until he saw my fae side come to life at the same time I learned how to shift. He couldn't look at me after that. I was too much like his mate, my mother. So he arranged for a mage to take over. He dropped me and my suitcase on Ness's doorstep one morning and I never saw him again.

Rage burns through my veins as the memory rises strongly to the surface. How someone could leave their child, especially a young one, is something I won't ever understand. Yes, my mom died, but I was still there. I was his blood. His last connection to her. Yet he tossed me aside like I meant nothing.

I finish packing everything, including that photo of my mom. Who knows what's going to happen next? If someone is after me, they could come here and destroy the place. I want my things with me. When done, I find the males in the same spot I left them in, talking about what they told the police and how they still have no idea who did it.

Don is the first to speak. "Solomon showed Tris the memory of where I'm staying with the clan, so he's going to teleport me back. Take care of yourself, Conni. And don't hide." He leans in and embraces me in a tight hug. The other males probably won't know what to think of his last comment, but I'm aware of its meaning. Don wants me to see if there's anything between Solomon and me.

I hide from most males. I don't touch them or let them touch me. I keep my heart closed off for fear of getting hurt.

I wrap my arms around the shifter and hold on to him like I won't see him again. I will, though. Once his father dies, he'll be back. He'll rebuild the bar. I'm just not sure when that will be. Until then, I'm stuck with a vampire. A very cocky one at that.

After giving Tristin a hug and Sol shaking hands with both males, Tris teleports Don away, leaving me alone with Mr. Full of Himself.

"Ready?" he asks.

"Depends. Are you going to touch me?"

"Well, I can't teleport you unless I have a hand on you. But rest assured, female, I won't let our skin touch. Fate forbid you find out if we actually have a connection." That's not the only reason I don't want our skin to touch, though it's the main one. I also don't want to accidentally let my emotions come through, thanks to my fae side.

I peer up at him in a moment of vulnerability. "Is that what you want?"

"What I want and what I get are rarely the same thing. I stopped dreaming of impossibilities a long time ago."

Something in Sol's voice causes my chest to ache. It's this tone of sadness that I haven't heard from him before. It makes me wonder how many layers there are to him.

I let his comment go for now and instead ask, "Where are we going?"

"Duck first. I have to pack as well and fill Ford in on what's going on. But I don't want to stay in the Outer Banks. That would be too logical. And given I have no clue who blew up the bar, I don't want to take any chances."

"Do you think whoever this is might be after me?"

He shrugs. "There's no way to tell yet. But since your life is very tightly wound with Don's, I don't want to take any unnecessary risks. He's back home with an entire clan of bear shifters. Tris will probably go to Ireland for a bit. That leaves you here with no family."

"I could go home to Canada."

"Yes, you could." He gives me a knowing look, no doubt having read my mind and learning about Vanessa.

"I did but only because I had to know who was up there. While the mage is very powerful, I would feel better protecting you myself." I love Ness, but I have a feeling Sol could protect me better than she could.

I try to lighten the mood and also get him off the topic of my past. "You never know. I might be the one who ends up protecting you."

"Or you'll be the one who hurts me worse than anyone else ever has," he says solemnly.

Okay, this conversation needs to come to an end. It's too deep in here, and I'm not in the mood to wade through painful memories and a bleak future, especially since it seems I'm not the only one with a tortured past.

Stepping up to Sol with my suitcase in tow, I wait for him to put his hand on my waist and teleport us away.

Instead of doing that, he trails the backs of his fingers from my clothed collarbone, down my side until finally resting his hand on my hip as his eyes follow the path. I suck in a breath, my body lighting up in a blaze of desire, but I can't move. I'm caught in his snare. And just when I think he might lean down and press his lips to mine, he snaps his fingers, bringing us to a bedroom.

"Real slick," I say. "And here I thought there was more to you than a cocky attitude and the need to get me in your bed."

Hurt flashes briefly across his face, but he's quick to school his features and replace the pain with a smirk. "If I wanted you between my sheets, believe me, I'd have you there. However, I happen to like this little game of cat and mouse we're playing. Or cat and vampire as it were. But in this game, the vampire always comes out on top." He winks and turns toward the closet.

Did he just make a sexual reference and turn away? How can one paranormal be so sexy and so frustrating at the same time?

"It's a skill," he calls out from the walk-in closet.

I groan in frustration and clench my fist not holding my suitcase. "Would you stay out of my head?"

"Stop projecting your thoughts about me and maybe I wouldn't hear every single thing which crosses that brain of yours."

I spin and stomp out of his room and down a hallway until I reach a set of stairs that takes me to the main living area. Three feet into the room I screech and jump in the air, my suitcase dropping to the ground in a loud thud. Standing before me is Sol's brother and a female I've never seen before.

"You really should announce yourself, brother!" Sol

yells from upstairs.

"I didn't think I had to." He focuses on me. "You're half shifter and half fae and you didn't hear us enter the home? We have to work on your skills. That should have never slipped by you."

"You didn't make any noise!" I yell defensively.

"I'm breathing, aren't I? Hence… noise." He cocks an eyebrow.

"You're as infuriating as your brother."

"Yes, he is," the female by his side cuts in. "Hi, we haven't met yet. I'm Sienna, Ford's mate." She offers me her hand, which I take while not letting my emotions flow from me to her, and shake.

"I'm Constance. It's nice to meet you."

"Don't mind Ford. Or Sol, for that matter. You won't find more loyal, protective males in the universe. They're good ones to have on your side."

Ford smiles down at his mate and presses a kiss to her forehead. "You're not so bad yourself."

"I am pretty awesome."

Sol appears suddenly next to me with a duffle bag slung over his shoulder. "I'm glad to hear you're embracing your Verascue name, Sienna. And we are awesome. The best of the best." He beams. I roll my eyes. No matter where we're going, it's going to be a long, trying trip.

# CHAPTER ELEVEN

*Solomon*

**AFTER GIVING MY BROTHER** A QUICK UPDATE of everything that happened, including our statement and story to the police, I use my mind to tell him where I'm taking Lilah, in case anyone is looking for me that I actually want to see. Like Wake, Paige, Ari, and so on. He nods and we say our goodbyes. Ford and Sienna teleport away.

"Are you ready?" I ask Lilah.

"Do I have a choice?"

I smile. "Not really." I watch as she fights the lift of her lips. I'm breaking down her walls. Soon I'll have her laughing and relaxed. Not so defensive, ready to beat my butt all the time.

I hold out my hand for her. She quirks an eyebrow in response. "Worth a shot," I tell her.

Clasping my hand on her shoulder, I make sure my duffle bag is secure on me and she's holding her suitcase, then I snap and teleport us to one of my many homes. We land in my living room and I try to take it in from someone else's point of view.

It's a large home: two stories, vaulted ceiling in this

room with high windows and a grey stone fireplace. The two couches in front of it in an L shape are tan suede. There's an area rug situated between them with a coffee table that is made out of reclaimed wood. The ceiling has long, broad exposed beams that give the room a rustic feel.

"This is beautiful," Lilah murmurs. "I was expecting more flash or something extravagant. I'm sure this place was expensive, but it's not overly done. It feels homey."

"I like each home to have a different vibe. I come here when I want to relax, especially in the winter." I love this home as much as the others.

"Where are we?"

"West central New Jersey."

Lilah walks over to the windows and peers outside. There are twenty acres surrounding the home, trees on all sides but with a cleared area between the house and the woods. It's very secluded. You can't see the road from the home, and I prefer it that way. I don't even plow the driveway in the winter since I don't need to drive anywhere here. The neighbors think I go south for the winter, so I let them believe that. They don't need to know when I show up here and they can't see me from their homes.

"Of all the places in the world, you take me to New Jersey," she mutters.

"There's nothing wrong with the Garden State. It gets a bad rep. So many have this vision of what Jersey is and it's not that. It's a great place with beaches, mountains, lots of land, and it's close to New York City and Philadelphia. There's so much to do."

"I have a feeling you don't do any of it, though."

"Hey, I go to the balloon festival when I can." Lilah laughs and I take a moment to watch her. She's beautiful when she relaxes. I'm keeping my distance, giving her space.

And it's doing good.

"I'm not mocking the state, just curious. It is very pretty here."

"It is and no one will bother us. If they do, I'll take care of them. Also, this should be the last place anyone looks for you. Only my family knows I have a home here. Come on. I'll show you around the house and then to your room."

"You're not going to try to get me to sleep in your bed?"

"My door is always open to you, kitten." I wink.

She shakes her head but follows me through the house as I show her the kitchen, dining room, formal living room, office, and then upstairs to the four bedrooms and three bathrooms. There's one additional bathroom downstairs. I pick the room closest to the master for Lilah. I might have some thoughts about what I'd like to do to her in bed, but the truth of the matter remains: there's someone out there. I'm not certain if they want to hurt her or Don, or maybe even Tristin. Don and Tris can handle themselves, though. Lilah might be able to as well. However, I'm making it my mission to keep her safe. Having her sleep in the room closest to mine will allow me to get to her quickly if need be.

Lilah places her suitcase on the king-sized bed and looks around the room. "I can't believe you own this house and the one in Duck."

"I have more than these. My family owns a villa in Italy. I also have homes in Florida, Australia, Greece, and Wyoming." I leave off a few others that I don't tell anyone about. My family is aware I have homes I never told them of, but they don't pry. Much.

"I can't imagine having the kind of wealth you do." She doesn't say it in a mean way but in a curious, resigned way.

"It's just money. My parents gave it to me. Same with Ford. We never have to work, but we can if we choose to. My mother can come off cold, but she and my father are very generous. They'd help out anyone in need. They'd also sever the head from anyone who dares to hurt who they love. Loyalty is never questioned in our family. We always protect one another, and we are always there if one of us is in need. When my brother's mate was in trouble, I took her and hid her in one of my homes. This, with you being here, is a bit like déjà vu, but this time it's better."

She cocks her head slightly to the side. "Why?"

"Because we hated each other and Sienna was draining the life from my brother. She was also ultimately the one who saved him, but that's a story for a different day."

"Did you bring her here?"

I shake my head. "No, I took her to my home in Florida." I'm not sure why I'm telling her this. Maybe because I want to trust her. Maybe because no matter how much she tries to tell herself she needs to steer clear of me, I can't seem to walk away. I'm a moth and she's my flame. It could also be because I've never had anyone whose loyalty was to me and not to my brother first.

Ford was the one who introduced me to the Avynwood Pack. He was the one who brought all the friends I now have into my life. Yes, I trust Wake, Kylest, and so many more, but none of them were my friends first. Lilah is different. She's not mine, however, she also doesn't know my brother well.

Lilah yawns, reminding me that neither of us have slept in a while. The sun has been up for a bit.

"I'm going to leave you to get some rest. There's a bathroom through there." I point to the door to my right. "There's food downstairs if you get hungry—all dry goods.

I need to do a grocery order. But that's after a nap. I'm quite tired." What I am is hungry and not for lunchmeat. I want to sink my fangs into Lilah's neck and taste the blood flowing through her veins that gives her life. But I won't, nor will I say that out loud, because that would pretty much guarantee she'd open a portal and hightail it out of here never to return.

I walk toward the door and tell her I'm in the room next door if she needs anything. With one last glance over my shoulder, I gently pull the door shut and go into my room with my duffle bag in tow.

*"I'll be here when you wake,"* she says in my mind. Without me even speaking she knew what I was feeling. Luckily, I have a strong block up in my mind that she can't break through, or she'd know just how much I desire her. Not only to drink her blood but to have her in my arms. To know what her skin feels like beneath my fingers. To have her all to myself.

*"I trust you,"* I reply. I do. I just hope she doesn't do something to break that trust.

In my room, I unpack quickly and throw myself down on the bed. I'm tired, but there is zero chance of me actually falling asleep. Not only because of the beautiful female in the room next to mine, who I can hear moving about, but because there is someone out there who wishes to harm her or Don or Tris. I can't let that happen. I know deep down that Lilah would be a formidable opponent, but depending on who this is, she might not be able to take them on alone. It could be more than one person or paranormal, for that matter. I'm not sure at this point.

After she sleeps for a bit, I'm going to feed us and have a talk with her. I have to find out about her past, her family, everything. This way I can tick people off the list of who could be suspects. If there are some on it who would want to harm her, well, I'll pay them a visit myself. One by one, I'll remove any threat to her.

Okay, I realize I'm treating her as I would if she were my mate, but I can't help it. I have no idea if she's mine or not. She won't touch me and there's no way she's going to let me drink from her. So I'm stuck in limbo, not knowing if she's someone special to me. But that's okay. I'll take what I can get at this point. It's better than she treated me when we first met. Any improvement is a good one.

I toss and turn for a while, listening to her even breaths as she sleeps. Hours pass before my eyes finally drift closed, but as soon as they do, a scream wrenches from Lilah and has me rushing from my room to hers. There I find Lilah sitting up in bed with the sheet clutched to her chest and wild eyes.

My fangs immediately descend as I scan the room. "Where?" I ask in a hard tone.

She looks at me for a moment with glazed eyes and shakes her head. There are no new scents in here. No signs of entry through the windows. No one came up the stairs or I would have heard them.

I walk to the side of the bed, but she doesn't track my movement. "Lilah?" No response. She must be dreaming. "Lilah, baby, lie back down." She listens and does as I ask, but I don't touch her for fear of startling her.

Once she's lying on the bed again, I decide not to leave the room, instead opting for the chaise lounge in front of one of the windows. My blood is still pumping wildly through my veins, thinking someone could have been in here. Luckily, it was nothing, but whatever Lilah dreamed about upset her.

A soft whimper comes from the bed. I glance over and

notice the sheet held tight in her fists as tears run down her face. I can't resist going to her and quietly get up. Carefully, I sit down on the bed by her side. I run my hand over her hip, careful not to touch her skin. I want to soothe her, but her arms are bare thanks to the tank top she's wearing, and the sheet is up to her chest.

"I'm here," I tell her softly. "I'm not going anywhere. You're safe."

After a couple of minutes, she settles, and the tears stop. It takes everything in me not to brush them away, but I need to respect her wishes. She doesn't want our skin to touch.

I can't seem to move back to the window, however, opting to lie down next to her, careful not to touch her again, only looking after her while she sleeps.

A couple more hours tick by like this, with me soothing her once more. It didn't take long before she settled back into a peaceful sleep. If this is all she lets me offer her in terms of comfort, I'll take it. Having a small piece of her is better than nothing at all.

My life hasn't been short. Fifteen hundred years is a long time to live. Yet I've never shared a bed with someone like I am with Lilah. It was always for a purpose. Usually a very dirty, X-rated one. And while I want that with her, I find myself desiring so much more. She's not your average paranormal. She's smart and tough. Independent and stubborn. She's complex and I want to know all of her.

# CHAPTER TWELVE

## *Lilah*

**I WAKE TO WARMTH** SURROUNDING ME like a blanket, except when I move, I realize that blanket is an arm and a leg over the sheet that covers me. And hot breath on my neck.

Immediately, I fly out of bed and spin around to face who was touching me, anger pouring off me in waves, my hands splayed at my sides ready to fight. And then I see my snuggler—Solomon.

He stretches, blinks a few times, and looks me up and down. "Not the usual greeting I get when in bed with a female."

"Your cockiness knows no bounds. Why are you in my bed?" I screech.

"I didn't plan to end up here, but you were having nightmares, and the only way I could soothe you was to keep rubbing you softly."

"Rubbing which part?" I growl.

Sol rolls his eyes. "Getting off on someone asleep isn't my thing, kitten. So you can rest your pretty little head." My skin flushes as I think about him rubbing against me. My cheetah stirs at the thought of it. No, we're not doing this. He's not someone we want to be intimate with.

"I don't have nightmares," I reply dismissively.

"You do. I'm not sure why you don't want to acknowledge them, but that was what was happening. And you had more than one." I groan and bury my head in my hands. I haven't had one in years. That freaking explosion must have dredged up everything in my mind. I don't even remember dreaming, let alone having nightmares.

When I was little, after being left to live with Ness, I had a lot of nightmares. It took a while, but eventually they stopped. Guess I'm back to reliving painful memories. Goodie for me.

Sol climbs out of bed and I avert my gaze, not wanting to take in the length of his sleep-rumpled self. He's gorgeous. There's no denying it. However, I'm not admitting that to him.

His lips quirk up. And I just did.

"I wish you didn't hear my thoughts all the time," I say. "No matter how strong of a block I put up, you can tear it down."

"One of the perks of being the firstborn to my parents. Although, I'm not actively strolling around in your mind. I just hear them as they float to me."

"Your brother doesn't have the same skill?"

"He does, but mine is stronger. He hates that." Sol chuckles.

"Lots of sibling rivalry, huh?"

"Yes and no. We used to fight a lot, but since Ari came into his life, we've gotten along much better. Our dynamic changed."

"Ari?" I'm not sure who he's talking about.

"I'm guessing you heard about the pack war that

happened recently." I nod. "Ariane, or Ari for short, was at the heart of it. She's the one who killed the shifter who started it. She's best friends with my brother, and her other best friend is mated to my best friend, who also happens to be another one of my brother's best friends." I think I need a graph to follow this.

"Is there going to be a test when we're done because you lost me after the first best friend reference."

"If you stick with me long enough, you'll meet the whole pack. Great shifters. There's even a cat pride I could introduce you to. They're also one of Lealla's." I'm not even going to ask who that is. I'll probably end up with a more complicated response. Instead, I focus on something else he said.

"I don't need a pride." The last thing I want is to be part of one, and for them to think they own me and can tell me what to do. I would never want to be put in that position. No one, alpha or not, will order me around.

Sol puts his hands up. "It was just a suggestion. You don't want to meet the fae prince. You don't want to meet the pride alpha. What do you want out of life, Lilah? Because running, closing yourself off, isn't living." I hate that in the little time since we've met, he's figured out so much about me and that's without him digging around my head.

"What about you?" I ask.

"What about me? Ask me anything you want, and I'll answer you honestly. I don't have much to hide." Much, but he has something. Then again, I have a ton, so who am I to argue the point?

"Why are you helping me?"

"Would you like the answer you want to hear or the real reason?"

"Aren't they one and the same?" He shakes his head. I'm already here with him, in his house. He's protecting me. I should find out the truth of why he's doing this. "The real reason."

He steps around the bed to stand in front of me. He's close but not close enough that our bodies are touching. "Because from the first moment I saw you, I knew there was something different about you. I'm not sure what it is, or what kind of connection we have, since you won't dare let our skin touch and vampires don't react that way to our mates. I'd have to ask Ford to be sure since his mate is a shifter."

He takes a breath as his eyes hold mine. "The thought of someone hurting you, trying to kill you, makes my blood boil. I'm not sure who is after you, if they are in fact targeting you, or if they are only using you to get to Don since he wasn't there when the bomb went off. But when I catch them, and I will, I will murder them with my bare hands." The ferocity in his words sends a shiver of fear down my spine. It's not that I'm afraid of Solomon. That's the furthest from the truth. It's the thought that there is someone out there trying to kill me or Don or Tris. I guess it hasn't really sunk in until now, and I'm left shaken.

I'm a tough paranormal, but I can be killed. Immortal or not, no matter what type of paranormal someone is, they have a weakness.

Sol steps closer and reaches up like he's going to touch my jaw. For a moment, I let my mind wander to what that would feel like. What it would be like to have his skin on mine, comforting me, pleasuring me. But I can't let that happen. Falling for him would make me more vulnerable than I've ever been.

I step back, out of his reach. Sol sighs and drops his

hand.

"Are you ever going to let me in or keep this invisible shield around yourself so no one can get close to you?" he asks.

"I don't need anyone."

"Yeah," he scoffs. "Neither do I." There's a tinge of sadness in his words. Some part of me hates hearing it. Solomon shouldn't be sad ever. He's attractive, protective, and kind, once you get past the ridiculous flirting and enormous ego. I have no doubt he'd be a great mate to someone.

Intense jealousy flares to life in me unlike anything I've ever felt, but I quickly push it away. Sol isn't mine. I have no claim on him.

"Come on," he says. "I'm going to grab the laptop, and we'll order food since we're going to be here a while. I'll have it delivered as soon as I can. In the meantime, you can flip through the takeout drawer and find us something for dinner."

I follow him downstairs without another word. He shows me to the drawer and tells me to pick, then hands me a pen and a pad of paper. He said he'll eat from any of them.

While I flip through the menus, he starts putting together a grocery order, asking what things I like to eat. Fortunately, there's a lot we have in common in the food department: red meats, cheeses, breads. But fruit and vegetables, I love them and Sol looks like I'm asking for garbage when I bring them up.

"I don't know how you eat that," he says and scrunches up his nose. "You're a cheetah not a rabbit."

"Just because I can shift into a cat doesn't mean I don't like to keep my body healthy."

He snorts. "You could smoke a pack of cigarettes a day

and drink your body weight in fae wine and it still wouldn't have any effect on your health."

"Sorry for being conscious about what I put in my body." Sol glances up at me and an unnamed emotion crosses his face then he goes back to the order.

On the one hand, I'd love it if he would open up and let me know what he thinks, so I didn't have to guess. On the other, that would make me a hypocrite because I'm not exactly volunteering up my life story over here or telling him just how attractive I think he is.

We sit in silence for a bit before I pick a local Italian place. I haven't eaten yet today and am in the mood for a big meal: chicken, pasta, and a salad. Sol looks over the menu to figure out what he wants then takes my written order and calls it in.

It arrives just as he's finishing up the grocery order. I get up to go to the door when he steps in front of me, keeping me from moving farther.

"I'll get it," he states.

"Do you really think someone came up to New Jersey and is posing as a food delivery person just to get to me?"

"The house is under a ward. The only way for someone to get in here at this point is if I asked Irus to amend his spell. You opening the door and venturing outside would put you in danger. He didn't ward the entire land. Just the house." Huh. I didn't even notice the ward when we showed up. And who's Irus? He throws names around like I have a clue who these paranormals are.

"Wait. If that's the case, how did I get here? Wouldn't I have been blocked as well?"

"Oh, ye of little faith. When you went downstairs in my house in Duck and found my brother, I placed a call to Irus, who teleported out here to change the ward to allow you through. Actually, he teleported to Duck first, saw you in my memories, then came here."

"I didn't hear any of that."

"Irus is pretty stealthy. That and my brother was right, we have to work on your skills. He should never have gotten the slip on you."

The doorbell rings again. "Can we pick apart my skills later? I'm starving."

"This isn't fun for me. I hate finding weaknesses when it comes to your power. You should have everything at the tips of your fingers. Be able to detect and defend easily. But we can talk about that later. I'll get the food."

Sol strides away to the front door, while I'm left standing in the open living room wondering how much I'll have to divulge to him before whoever is after one of us is caught. My personal life? What I can and can't do? That would leave me vulnerable. I have a strong feeling I can trust Solomon with my life, but he's still new to me. Not like Don, who I've known for years, and who I wouldn't second-guess to talk to about anything. He's always there for me.

But being here with Sol puts a whole other layer into this already screwed-up situation. There's the attraction between us. He feels it. I feel it. So what am I going to do about it? Nothing. I can't. We need to find who blew up the bar and tried to hurt me so I can go back to the life I love. Or like. I'm not really sure I've ever loved anything about my life. I was content. Getting through each day the best I could while trying to keep my demons at bay.

Does anyone ever get over being abandoned by a parent? The death of another one? I didn't just lose one; I lost both before I turned five. If not for Vanessa, I'm not sure what would have happened. She was kind and nurturing. Maybe that's why my dad left me there. Or maybe it's because she was the first paranormal he could think of.

She wasn't new to me. She'd been our neighbor and my occasional babysitter when my dad would go out after my mom was gone. I can't imagine what must have gone through her head when I was dropped off and she had to spend years taking care of me. She doesn't regret a moment of it. She's told me repeatedly. But I still wish I'd grown up with both of my parents.

I don't miss my dad. He left, so I don't waste tears on him. But my mom? I miss her every day and can't help but imagine what my life would have been like if she hadn't died giving birth to me.

It's no wonder I'm having nightmares again. Being with Sol is causing me to dredge up memories I try to keep buried.

# CHAPTER THIRTEEN

## *Solomon*

**I COULD TELL LILAH** DIDN'T WANT TO TALK. Not a word was spoken through dinner. The grocery order wasn't supposed to arrive until the morning. So basically, there wasn't anything to do, except watch television or stare at each other. Don't get me wrong; I could stare at her night and day. The problem was getting my body on the same page since staring wasn't enough for it. My fingers itched to touch her. To thread into her hair while my lips press kisses along her jaw and throat. And the rest of my body? Let's just say there were lots of ideas it had of ways it could pleasure Lilah.

Two hours later and there's nothing on television. It's the same stuff over and over. I don't bother with the news or with what's popular. It's another reason I love my house in Duck. I can sit on the deck for hours just listening to the people there or the waves lap at the shore.

"Do you want to go for a walk?" I blurt out. I can't stand to sit here any longer and listen to the two people on television whine about whatever superficial problem they have. If they lived in our world, where death and violence reigned, they'd be in for a ton of pain.

"Um, sure," she replies. "I thought only the house was warded, though."

"It is, but you're with me and I'm like ten paranormals rolled into one, so there's no need to be afraid."

Her eyes narrow. "I wasn't afraid in Nags Head. It was you, Don, and Tris who thought it would be better if I were someplace else."

I wave her off. "Doesn't matter now. You're with me, and I'm bored. Let's go for a stroll."

She huffs in annoyance but puts her shoes on. I put mine on as well and we exit out the front door. I turn toward the street, but Lilah turns toward the back of the house. "Where are you going?" I ask.

"I thought you mentioned a trail or something back here."

"I did, but I don't want to walk on it. I'm not in the mood to get a thousand bug bites."

"You'll heal."

"Yes, physically, but the toll those little bloodsuckers take on me emotionally can't be undone."

"You hear yourself, right?"

I smile. "I always do."

We start down the long driveway until we come to the end where it meets the street. I open the mailbox, surprised to find a bunch of mail stuffed into it. I really should check this more often. Not that I get actual mail. It's all junk and the local township flyers that have built up for months. I shove it back in and turn left with Lilah at my side.

The road the house is on is quiet, not a lot of traffic. It's got a slight incline.

"You realize you can get bit by a mosquito out here, too, right?" she asks.

"Yeah, but if you go into the woods there are more of them than out here in the open."

"Your logic makes no sense."

I shrug. "That's okay. It doesn't need to."

"I've never met anyone like you." I don't miss the sound of the smile in her voice.

"Is that a good thing?"

"Yes and no." For a moment, I don't think she's going to elaborate, but then she starts to speak again. "It's a good thing because as much as I hate to admit it, I find you intriguing. It's a bad thing because I never know what you're going to say. At least when you came into the bar, I had some notion of how it would go when I spoke to you. You'd hit on me, drink nothing but water, and stare at me."

"I fail to see how that's different here."

"Stop trying to be funny for one second." Okay, so we're having a serious talk now. Right here in the middle of nowhere. Sure. Why not.

"Anyway," she continues. "You haven't relentlessly hit on me since we got here. Granted, it hasn't been that long, but you're usually quick with a pick-up line that I immediately shoot down. But this is different. I'm seeing another side of you. I'm not sure if you're doing it intentionally, or if you're finally relaxing a little around me and not bothering to put up a facade." I open my mouth to counter, but she holds her hand up. "Before you can say you don't do that, you do. I wonder if it's like me. It's a wall you've built so not everyone can get to know the real you. Although, I have a feeling you let some in. Like your brother and his mate. Ari and your other friends."

I let her statement go without a response and ask, "Who do you let in?"

"Don."

"No one else?"

"Vanessa, I guess. Not with everything, though." I watch her curiously until she elaborates. "She raised me from a small child after my dad decided he didn't want me." I have a feeling if I let this go without asking any questions, she won't offer up the information again. I want to know all of her, and this is my chance.

"What happened?"

"My dad is a cheetah shifter and my mom was fae. They fell in love and mated. She got pregnant with me then died while giving birth. My dad couldn't handle it when my powers started to surface. He wanted me to be a pure shifter, but my fae side came through at the same time. I reminded him too much of my mom, so he left me with Vanessa." I want to reach out and pull her into my arms. To tell her I won't abandon her like he did. Because I have a feeling deep down that's where a lot of her problems lie. She doesn't get close to anyone for fear of them leaving her. I can't blame her. She lost both parents. But I'm not a male who gives up on others and dismisses them. And more than anything else, I understand what it's like to feel alone.

"I'm sorry that happened to you."

She shrugs. "Me, too. I wish I still had my mom. I never got to have what so many other children do. And my dad, what memories I have of him, are mixed. Sure, there were times when he was good to me. He took me on trips; we had fun. He never hit me or called me names. But any good part evaporated when he noticed my mom's fae side in me." I decide a change of subject is in order.

"Tell me about Vanessa."

She cocks her head. "Why do you want to know?"

"I like hearing about your life. It helps me understand why you are the way you are and where you came from."

She studies me for a moment before speaking. "Vanessa has been an amazing influence on me. She wasn't sure what to do with a half shifter/half fae child, but she brought friends over to teach me as time went on. She also taught me some basic spells, though I can do more with my fae magic, so I rely on that. She was never harsh or cold. Completely opposite of that. Her home was always warm and inviting. Even when I go back now, she's there to welcome me with open arms. She's been a steadfast presence in my life. Someone who I treasure and am grateful for."

"She sounds like a great female."

"She is." She smiles. "Your turn."

I groan but ultimately tell Lilah the abbreviated version of my life. How I've been to a lot of places. Raised in a loving family, despite how cold my mom can be to others. How my father balances her out.

Then I get to Ford. "I'm trusting you with something," I start. "I'd appreciate anything I tell you to stay between us." She nods and I take a leap by divulging things I've never told anyone. "I was an only child for a long time. It was great. I had both of my parents' attention. It was all I knew. Then Ford came along. It wasn't easy adjusting to having a brother. Our family dynamic changed. A lot of my parents' attention focused on him, as it should have. But I was jealous.

"Yes, I was an adult and had been for quite some time, but to have my world flipped upside down by gaining a brother threw me. I shut down. Ford, however, didn't like it when I ignored him. We'd fight. A lot. I never voiced how I felt. I'm a Verascue after all, and we don't show vulnerability. Once Ari came along, everything changed. I also realized how quickly and easily I could lose the only brother I had. I didn't want that. He's my blood and I'd die for him. We're close now. Freakishly so. We still fight as any siblings would, but we have each other's backs. We're tight."

A lot of paranormals see my family name or my brother or me and think of nothing but the power we have. It's what draws females in, but there's so much more to us. The problem is that not many bother to see it. They want the notoriety that comes with being with a Verascue, while all I want is someone to share my life with.

If there were one thing my mom drilled into our heads from a young age, it was that we don't ever force love. We don't settle. We wait until our fated mate appears, and we give them our whole heart. Too bad my brother had to suffer all he did while everything happened with Sienna. But I'm sure if I asked him if he had to do it all over again to end up where he is, he would certainly do it.

The love he and Sienna have is something I want. I want a female to look at me with hearts in her eyes and only see me. Not my name. Not my bloodline. Not the power I can give her. Just me—Solomon Verascue—with all my faults, insecurities, and issues.

I think that could be Lilah. The problem is her testing the waters to see if it is. I haven't told her, but she could never be a conquest to me. She's already much more than that. Not only a friend, which I consider her regardless of how she sees me.

We finally turn around and head back toward the house as I tell her about Ari, Orion, Lealla, the rest of the pack, and the war that took place. She knows some of it, hearing details from Donovon but he wasn't there. I'm able to fill in the gaps and tell her what happened and how it all came to an end. I also tell her about the lives lost along the way.

I might not have been close with everyone who died, but they should be remembered. They died so others could continue fighting and secure peace for North Carolina.

For the short life Lilah has lived so far, she was fortunate that she never crossed paths with Travis. I'm glad she was spared and the fight never came to the Outer Banks, or worse, spread to other areas of the country. To think of a world where I wouldn't have met her sends a sharp pain through my chest.

When we finally turn the corner into the driveway, darkness blankets us and the moon is high above. I don't want to go back inside. I don't want to break the spell we're under. We've both opened up and there's something freeing about it. Going back inside could shatter that. Lilah could clam up, and then I'll be left wondering how to get her to talk to me again.

I've never been as invested in someone as I am in her. If only I could hold her when we get inside. All I want to do is keep her by my side where she's safe. Would she be comfortable with me? She's more relaxed than she's been in my presence. I'll take it as a good sign.

We reach the door but before I can open it, she turns to me. "I had a surprisingly nice time tonight."

"Is it that hard to believe I'm not a completely shallow male with one thing on my mind?"

"No, but you come off that way. I'll make you a deal. You don't hide who you truly are, and I won't either."

"Deal." I smile and hold out my hand. She hesitates, looking down at what I'm offering. For a moment, I don't think she's going to accept it, but then she does.

Lilah's warm palm slides into mine and she gasps as her eyes lift to meet mine. Then she immediately drops it and steps back. There's only one reason for that reaction.

"We're mates, aren't we?" I ask. Not every mate bond between a vampire and a shifter will work the same. For us, she must feel the spark.

She nods then shakes her head. "I can't do this, Sol. I can't have a mate. So much could go wrong. So many emotions could get mixed in and then what? What happens when you decide I'm too young for you or I'm not enough? What happens when I don't live up to everything you've always thought your mate would be?" I want to pull her into my arms, however, decide against it. She's already freaking out. I don't want to make it worse.

"Lilah, I'm not like the males who've hurt you. I'm not someone who leaves their friends or family behind. You don't fully trust me yet, and I get that. I'm going to prove to you that I'm a male worthy of your attention and affection."

# CHAPTER FOURTEEN

## *Lilah*

**MY WHOLE WORLD IS SPINNING**—TILTED ON its axis—thanks to the male in front of me. I didn't want this to happen. I didn't want a male tied to me. I meant it when I said there's a lot that could go wrong. He's fifteen hundred years old and I'm nineteen. Talk about an age gap. He's freaking ancient in the body of a twenty-five-year-old.

"Lilah, I know you're not exactly on board with this," Sol says carefully.

"On board? How can I be on board with it when I've been actively trying to avoid it since I was old enough to understand what a mate was?" With every word, my voice gets higher. I'm bordering on hysterics. Not only is my life in danger, but I also have a freaking mate. A vampire mate! One who is of the purest bloodlines among all the vampires. Holy fate, I'm going to become some sort of vampire royalty.

"Well, not royalty." Sol grins. "More like you'll be the envy of every female out there."

"Seriously?" I shout. "For one second can you not let your ego inflate your head?" Man, this vampire. And he's my fated mate for all of eternity. Sounds about right. Nothing in my life is half-hearted. If I'm going to have a mate, it may as well be Sol.

"Hey," he says softly, pulling me back to the present. "We don't have to seal the bond. We don't have to become mated." My stomach drops as a sick feeling settles in it.

"Is that what you want?" I said I never wanted a mate, but to hear the words come from Sol that we don't have to seal the bond; is that how he felt when I said them? Does he think this is personal to him? I've royally screwed this up.

His voice is tentative when he speaks. "It doesn't matter what I want." The hurt in his eyes has emotion clogging my throat. I put that there. The male who risked his life when mine was in danger, then brought me to this safe place. He really does deserve better than me.

I step close to him so I can lay my palms on his chest and peer into his eyes. "I never wanted a mate. You're aware of my past. I'm sure you can understand why. My words weren't meant to be personal to you. I'm reeling at the discovery that you're mine." Solomon Verascue is my mate. This blond Adonis of a male is the one I'm fated to spend the rest of my immortal life with.

"I want to be yours, Lilah." My given first name on his lips doesn't bother me anymore. Sol has used it from day one. Maybe his mom was right. I need to embrace it and not let the past shroud my future.

"Can you give me some time? I need to wrap my head around this. I'm not saying no. More like yes, but with some conditions we need to discuss. Plus, there's the whole someone out to kill me or Don or Tris business to sort out." Did I seriously just agree to be his mate? So much for thinking things through. I went from asking for time to agreeing to it within seconds. My mouth is running faster than my brain. Lovely.

Sol opens his mouth to speak as his fangs descend. “No one will kill you, Lilah. You’re mine. Forever.”

With that, he dips his head and presses his lips to mine. There, that spark of our touch amplifies and sends electricity through my body as his tongue brushes over the seam of my lips. I immediately open for him.

Never in my life have I been kissed. Never have I been held in the arms of a strong male with passion. Not only is the mate part new to me, but having someone kiss and touch me is brand-new territory as well.

Slowly, I pull back and meet his eyes. I have to be honest. There’s no other way to be at this point. “You’re my first kiss.”

“If you allow me, I want to be your first everything.” I let out a breathy sigh. How did this male go from making me want to escape his giant ego to saving my life to having me utterly swooning for him?

Sol smacks his hand to his neck. “Son of a!” He pulls it away and there is a crushed mosquito on it. “See! Bloodsuckers!” He turns to yell into the night. “You better run now because I’m going to order a bug zapper to fry you suckers!”

I laugh and open the door at my back to pull him inside. “Let’s get you safe before the mean bugs steal more of your blood.”

“Hey, I have prime blood. Legends are made of the stuff pumping through my veins. They should be so lucky to dine on a delicacy such as me.” He kicks the door shut behind him and locks the deadbolt before setting the alarm.

“Why didn’t you lock up and set that before we left?”

He cocks his head in thought. “I completely forgot. I

was too focused on you, kitten." He shakes his head and scans our surroundings. "That won't happen again."

"You're an old, powerful vampire and you need an alarm on your house?"

"You make it sound like I'm about to get a walker and bigger shoes for balance. I do it so I have another layer of protection." I open my mouth, but Sol puts up a hand to stop me. "And don't bring up again how I forgot it. Even with the ward, I'd rather be safe than sorry. Plus, when I'm not here, I'll be alerted if some human tries to steal from me."

"You're not hiding the Crown Jewels in here, Sol."

"My jewels are way more precious than those of any royal family."

"We were having a moment outside and now everything you say is full of innuendo."

He smiles. "Get used to it."

I pat him on the shoulder. "Okay, you think of more things to say while I go upstairs and shower then crawl back into bed. I thought I wouldn't be ready for sleep so soon, but I still have some to catch up on. I'll see you in the morning." With that, I turn and start up the stairs.

"Lilah?" he calls quietly.

I stop and peer over my shoulder. "Yeah?"

"I'm here. I'm not going anywhere. All you have to do is say my name and I'll be there for you."

"You're a good male, Solomon Verascue. Even if you have the biggest head in the universe."

"All the better to hear you with, my dear." I roll my eyes and continue up the stairs.

When I enter my room, I close the door behind me and strip before stepping in the shower. For a few minutes, I simply stand there and try to wrap my head around everything that's happened. Not just with the explosion but with Sol.

I have a mate. I can hardly believe it. It figures fate would give me one when I least expect it and when I didn't want one. Then again, I don't think fate cares one way or another about what any of us wants.

The question becomes, what next? I'm not ready to seal our bond. I only had my first kiss tonight. The last thing I want is to jump into bed with him. Though, the idea of going to sleep and waking up with his arms wrapped around me is appealing. I woke up that way before, but I didn't get a chance to soak it in, thanks to the fact that he scared me by being there.

I wish I had someone to talk to about this. Someone who would understand what I'm going through and help guide me. As much as I love Ness, she isn't mated. I could talk to Ford's mate, although, I don't know her and she might look at me differently because Sol is her family.

I wash my hair and body then rinse. The towels Sol has are soft and as light as air. Not that I expected anything different. Nothing of his is poor quality.

After slipping into a pair of shorts and a tank top, I crawl into bed and lie on my side so I can peer out the windows. I never bothered closing the blinds. It's a clear night with stars twinkling overhead and the moon casting a sliver of its light into the room.

What am I doing? My life has never been easy, and I've never done what was asked of me. With the exception of being removed from my home at the age of four, everything has been on my terms. Yet I'm considering allowing a male into my life. Will he try and take control over things? Tell me what to do? That would never work. I'm not that kind of female. Then again, nothing about Sol tells me he's the pushy, dominating type. Sure, he's a total alpha, but not in a bad way. I don't think he'd restrict me, only look out for me.

After tossing and turning for a bit, my eyelids finally feel heavy and sleep claims me.

****

I'm awoken in the morning to the sounds of birds chirping out the window and the gentle rustling of leaves as the wind lightly blows through the trees. There's also a very warm body pressed to my back, who is no longer being careful about where he touches me, as evidenced by his hand twined with mine around my stomach. Those sparks are there, reminding me that this isn't just anyone. This is my mate, even if we aren't officially bonded yet.

I let his hand go and roll over in his arms. His blond hair is standing up and his eyes are closed. But I can tell by his breathing and the beat of his heart that he's no longer asleep.

His eyes open, piercing me with that grey color I've only seen in his family. "Morning, kitten." He places a soft kiss on my nose.

"Was I having a nightmare again?"

He nods. "Four times. You aren't angry that I'm here?"

"No. I thought about what it would be like to sleep in your arms last night. You know, when I'm not rocketing out of bed out of fear of who's touching me."

"I would have come to you. All you had to do was call."

Reaching up, I brush a wayward strand of hair from his forehead. My touch creating sparks under my fingertips as it goes. "I needed time to process."

"And?"

"I want to be yours, Sol, but I can't help be worried. I'm not sure how to handle this."

"I have a friend who is recently mated. His female was worried about losing him. Her father died when she was young, and she didn't want to lose her mate. Would it help if you talked to her? She's young like you. Didn't meet her mate under the best circumstances but is now blissfully happy."

"I'd actually like that. But I'd want to talk to her alone. I don't need you or her mate there listening to everything."

"Whatever you're most comfortable with. I'll arrange it once we get out of bed." He wraps both arms around me and pulls me against him until my head rests under his chin.

"We can get up now," I say as I nestle in closer, soaking up his warmth and touch.

"I hear so much conviction in your voice," he replies sarcastically. I pinch his side, causing him to squirm. "Don't do that, you evil female."

"You haven't seen evil yet."

"Is it wrong that I'm torn about ever seeing that side of you?" I'm not sure what he's getting at. "On one hand, if you're that angry it means something's going down, and I don't want you anywhere near conflict. On the other, I'm completely turned on by the idea of your cat coming out and tearing into someone."

"I'm not surprised by this one bit." That reminds me… "Can we go out into the woods today? I want to shift and let my cheetah run. She's been cooped up and while she's okay for a little bit, I can feel her getting restless inside me. I also think she wants to meet you."

"We certainly can. I'd like to meet her as well. You know, as long as she doesn't try to sever my head with one of her claws."

I smile. "If you're my mate, she wouldn't dare take a swipe at you. I think she wants to be sure. It's one thing to feel the connection through me and another to get up and personal with you."

"By personal you mean…"

"Sniff you, get in your face. Honestly. Your mind always goes to a dirty place."

He grins. "I can't help it. I've been a wild male for far too long. You're going to have your work cut out for you trying to tame me." My body tenses in his hold. I don't want to hear about the other females he's been with.

"You won't speak of the females you've taken to bed, and I won't tell you about the males who've hit on me." His fingers tighten on my hip. I'm not the only jealous one. At least the playing field is even.

"Deal."

# CHAPTER FIFTEEN

*Solomon*

**LATER THIS AFTERNOON,** I HAVE PLANS for Lilah. But right now, we're walking to the woods where I'm going to be introduced to her cheetah.

There was a time in my life when I wasn't a fan of shifters. But then Ford met Ari, and I met Ari, and everything changed. Now my best friend is a wolf shifter and I wouldn't have it any other way.

I've learned a lot about shifters. There isn't one attitude that covers them all. The more I meet, the more I see. Each pack is different. Each member of the pack has their own personality, not like they're sheep blindly following one leader. Yes, they will yield to the alpha, but in the packs I've grown to learn about, there is no powerful male leading them saying they have to do everything he orders. The alphas aren't strict, yet they know when needed, their pack will be there. There's a lot of freedom in it. It's a family. A tight knit group of paranormals who find a home with each other.

We enter the tree line and go a little deeper, just in case.

Lilah turns to face me. Her brown hair is down around her shoulders. She's wearing a pair of very small shorts and a tight tank top, which I happen to greatly appreciate, and flip-flops. She said she didn't see any point in wearing anything else out there. I miss her high heels. She can't wear them in the woods, though. They're more for work and if she goes out. Maybe if we ever mate, I'll be able to convince her to wear them in bed and nothing else.

She claps her hands in my face. "Hello? Earth to Solomon?"

"Sorry, kitten. I imagined you in a particular outfit and it made me very happy."

She crosses her arms. "Uh huh. And was this outfit actually not an outfit and, in fact, me naked?"

"It was." I smile. "Well, you had your heels on." She rolls her eyes.

"My cat is getting antsy, so I'm going to shift."

"There are other ways to take care of your kitty."

"You really know no bounds."

"Nothing coming out of my mouth should shock you at this point."

"It's not that. Just this never-ending stream of dirty thoughts." I nod and smile. "Okay, on that note…"

Lilah takes a few steps back. Her eyes flash sapphire a second before she shifts from her gorgeous self into a tall, sleek cheetah. Her animal's eyes are on me, looking me over from head to toe. She begins a slow stroll around me while I wait to see what she does next. She's about three feet at the shoulder and roughly four feet long. I've never seen an animal so beautiful.

Her cheetah stops in front of me and sits down. I'm not quite sure what I'm supposed to do, and Lilah isn't exactly talking to me telepathically, so I go off instinct and sit on the ground as well.

I'm not scared of her. Since we're mates, there's no way her cheetah is going to hurt me. At least I hope not. She stands again, but this time gets right in my face to sniff my nose then my neck, and pads behind me to sniff my hair. I'm going to need a shower after this. Cat slobber all over me.

The cheetah hisses, reminding me to keep my thoughts in check.

"What?" I ask. "If nothing else, I'm honest."

*"She might not be able to hear your thoughts, but she felt your mood shift,"* Lilah says in my mind.

"Nice of you to join us," I droll.

*"Oh shut up and spend time with her."*

"I'm not sure what I'm supposed to be doing."

*"Let her lead."*

"Thank you. That's exactly what I've been doing."

The cheetah walks in front of me then steps over my legs before settling down on my lap. Didn't expect that.

Once she's comfortable, she rests her head on her front paws, and I take a moment to look over the cat on me. No, she doesn't fit on me, but she made herself at home. Gently, I lift my hand and stroke the fur on her back. A soft purr vibrates through her. Who would have thought something so big and powerful would want to be mine?

We sit like that for a while. Me stroking her fur and her purring contentedly. Lilah remains quiet and I do as well, taking my time to get to know her cheetah.

She eventually stirs and stands at my side, so I rise from the ground as well.

"You should go for a run. It's quiet out here. I don't hear anyone around. Just stick to the trees and come back. I don't want to have to go all over New Jersey looking for you." The cheetah eyes me curiously then turns and takes off at a speed I've never seen any shifter go.

I'm not sure what to do with myself now. It's not like I have a packed schedule. Yes, I have something going on this afternoon, but I still have an hour or so until that. My stomach growls, deciding for me.

Walking toward the house, I enter through the sliding doors at the back and leave them open so if Lilah wants to come in, or her cheetah, she'll know where I am. Not that I want her cheetah walking around without the cover of the forest, but I doubt she'd listen to me. I'll be amazed if she stays in there now. The last thing I need is the cops showing up, telling me how a cheetah escaped from the local zoo and to lock myself inside. The vision of them trying to tranquilize her appears in my head. That'll go over real well. I can see the headline now, *"Cheetah Severs Arm of Animal Control Officer. Tranq Gun Not Effective."*

I'm glad I decided to head back to the house when I did. I forgot about the grocery order, which arrives five minutes later.

The entire time the young guy who helps me walks back and forth to his vehicle, I'm scanning the tree line, waiting for a jungle cat to pounce. I told him I'd unload them myself, but he insisted it's part of his job and he doesn't want his manager finding out he didn't do as he should. I let him do his thing, however, he's only allowed to go so far. I take the bags from him and bring them inside so he doesn't have to. After a generous tip, he's gone.

As I'm walking back into the house, I see Lilah emerge from the backyard. She looks the same as she did going in, but her eyes are a little brighter now. The run did her some good.

"Go anywhere interesting?" I ask.

"Not really. My cheetah found a creek and stalked a deer. Of course, she caught it and ripped into it like no one's business. We might have to go back out there and hide the carcass. I don't want someone stumbling upon it."

I wave her off. "There have been coyote sightings near here. I'm not worried. Besides, whatever your cheetah didn't eat will be a nice snack for the other predators out there."

My stomach growls again.

"Hungry?" she asks.

"Yes, and we have groceries now. What are you in the mood for?"

"I'm easy. That deer only satisfied her, not me. I'll take whatever you're having."

"Sooo me on the table wearing nothing but a smile?"

"You're relentless."

I step to her and loop my arm around her back to bring her to me, unable to help myself. Her hands land on my chest as she smiles up at me. "Only where you're concerned."

"You've never pursued a female like you have me?"

I shake my head. "Nope. If they aren't interested in me from the start, I leave them alone. Solomon Verascue does not beg anyone to come home with him."

"Except me."

"You are the exception to that rule."

She places a quick kiss on my lips then extracts herself from my arms. I'm not certain as to where her head is at. Yes, she said she wants to be with me, but I won't push her into it. I don't want her to one day regret that we're mated. This could be the female I'm going to spend the rest of eternity with. I need her to be certain.

Lilah walks over to the counter and helps me unpack.

She lifts two packages of lunch meat and three of cheese. "I'm guessing you like sandwiches."

"I like not cooking. Sandwiches are easy and portable."

"Do you often walk around eating a sandwich?"

"You'd be surprised."

Once everything is put away, we stand at the counter side by side and make sandwiches, then add pickles to our plates before sitting at the table. Surprisingly, the lunch conversation is kept light. No talk of someone possibly after her or the fact that fate decided I'm her mate. It's nice talking without any added pressure.

We're just finishing when there's a knock on the front door. Lilah looks at me inquisitively. I don't answer her unasked question and stride to the door. When I open it, there's the fae prince and his fae mate.

Kylest is wearing a pair of khaki shorts and a sky blue T-shirt. Today, his hair is a burnt orange with black tips. This male and his fashion sense. His female is in a matching outfit of khaki shorts that hit mid-thigh and a sky blue tank top. Her hair brushes her shoulders and is at least a solid shade of black.

"Your hair clashes with your shirt," I tell Kylest.

"Thank you!" Raven exclaims. "That's exactly what I said. He wouldn't listen. Said he felt like wearing soothing colors but was keeping his hair ready for a rave. I'm not even sure raves are still a thing in the mortal world."

"I only leave the house to get into trouble or pick up females," I tell her.

"They're one and the same where you're concerned," Lilah pipes up behind me. "You going to keep them on the doorstep?" She comes to stand by my side.

"Right. Come in. No reason to stand outside amongst the bugs." They cross into the house easily. I had the forethought to add Ky and Raven to the ward when I saw Irus. Not that I knew I'd ask them to come over, but I never want them to feel unwelcome in my home. The fae prince and princess are powerful allies to have.

Once inside, they both drop their glamour and let their natural skin and ears show through.

Lilah gasps. "You're both fae." She whirls on me. *"Is there a reason you didn't tell me you invited members of the fae over? Are you trying to make me crazy?"*

*"I think that ship sailed when we first met."*

She groans loudly in my mind. *"Be serious."*

*"You said you wanted someone to talk to who might understand what you're going through. Well, this is who you can talk to. They're newly mated and Raven lost her dad when she was younger. She was worried about Kylest abandoning her."*

"Not abandoning," Raven interjects, reading our minds to hear our conversation. "I was worried something was going to happen to him and he wouldn't come back. He left one time and never told me. I woke up scared and full of fear."

Kylest rests his hand at the small of his mate's back. "I didn't make that mistake again."

"So, you both can hear our conversation, even though we have blocks up?" Lilah asks.

"Being fae royalty has its perks." Kylest winks.

"Holy fate." She turns to me with anger in her eyes. "You not only invited fae here to talk to me but a prince and princess?"

I lean to the right to peer at our guests. "I'd like to say she usually isn't like this, but that would be a lie. She has a lovely temper."

"You haven't seen my temper yet," she growls.

"I like her," Kylest states with a smile.

Lilah turns to face them. "I apologize for my behavior. Solomon likes to ambush me with things and never feels bad about doing so."

"That's not true," I say defensively. "I wouldn't have made you leave your home if I thought there was a better, safer way."

"Whatever," Lilah scoffs. "You would have done about anything to get me in your bed."

"And I won."

"No," she says pointedly. "You ended up in my bed."

Raven laughs. "I like this pairing a lot."

"Me, too," Kylest agrees. "I think you've met your match, Sol."

"Isn't that the point of mates?" I ask.

"So, you are destined then, but not yet mated?" Kylest asks.

"No. That's one of the reasons I asked you here. I was hoping Lilah could spend some time with Raven and they could talk about it. Not the details of what happens, but they're both the same age, and we're both…"

"Old," Kylest adds with a chuckle.

"I was going to say distinguished, but whatever."

He laughs loudly. "I love you, Sol, but distinguished wouldn't be the first word I used to describe you."

My eyes narrow at him. "Why are we friends again?" His only response is to keep laughing. Freaking fae prince.

# *Lilah*

**AT FIRST, I WAS MAD AT SOL.** WELL, ONLY A LITTLE. I did say I wanted someone to talk to, but a fae prince and princess? Seriously? Of all the mated pairs in the world, this is who he asks to visit me.

After introductions are officially made, Raven says, "I want you to come with me. I think we need a break from the testosterone and egos."

"Yours, too?" I ask.

She smirks. "You have no idea."

We make our way upstairs to the bedroom I've been using. Inside, Raven closes the door. She removes a bracelet from her wrist and flicks it into the air. The bracelet expands and a portal opens, but it's veiled in silver. I can't see on the other side. If Sol wouldn't have invited them here personally, no way would I go—but he did—and that must mean he trusts them.

"If you try to kill me," I begin, "I'll rip you apart."

"I have no doubt you'll try, but you won't succeed. You're not mated to Solomon yet. When you are, then you might come close to being able to take me."

"Our males aren't the only cocky ones."

She winks. "Touché."

Raven steps through first and I follow. I've traveled via portals for years, but trusting someone else, when you can't see the other side, is a huge leap.

I step through to a big open room with a throne on one side. Raven grips the bracelet and closes the portal.

"Ignore the throne," Raven says. "I do. It should be at the palace, but Ky likes it here where he can keep it safe. He gets so angry when I use it to store things. Like the other night, we had guests over and I had no place to put a bowl of mashed potatoes, so I sat it on the throne." She starts laughing. "You should have seen the look on his face. He would have been happier if I'd killed someone."

"Man, you're weird."

She rights herself, still smiling. "I embrace my weirdness. If you've seen all I have, you'd be weird, too." She walks to the kitchen. "Do you want anything to drink? Eat?"

"No, I'm good."

"Okay, then let's sit and talk before Sol tries to force Ky to bring him here. I'm sure he isn't happy we left, but Ky will reassure him."

"Where is here exactly?"

"We're not in the mortal realm but not in the fae realm either. We're in the in-between. It's a space between realms where Ky and I live. It's quiet here and not many paranormals know about it, so we're left alone a lot."

"Don't you have land to rule?"

"Yes, we rule North America, but we don't have to be there all the time. In fact, we're not there much. We're hermits for the most part."

"Doesn't that get isolating? I'd think you'd be lonely."

I can't imagine being cut off from everyone. It's not like there's a town here where they can walk down the road and grab a pizza. Or go hang out with friends.

"You'd think so, but once you're mated, you realize your mate is the only one you'll ever truly need. Plus, things can get a little loud, if you know what I mean, so here we can shout at the top of our lungs and no one hears us."

"I think that's more information than I needed." In truth, this is relaxing me. Making the conversation flow a little better. It's easy.

"Okay, so let's get down to business. Sol told Ky that you're nervous about being mated. I can understand that. My dad died when I was younger. I won't go into details because that's not important to the topic at hand. When I first met Ky, he was looking for his sister. She was missing and there were next to no clues about her whereabouts. So Ky and his family searched every inch of the mortal realm, as well as others, and since I was living in Ky's territory in Texas, he was at my house doing a check, seeing if we knew anything. I volunteered my help and now we're mated. That's the abbreviated version. You don't need all the details about what happened to his sister, but before you ask, yes, she's alive." Raven takes a breath but keeps talking. Is this what happens when you don't have people to talk to for long stretches of time? You have to remember to suck in a breath when you speak at the speed of sound?

"Anyway," she continues. "I was scared. Here I was a common fae, and I mean common. There wasn't a bit of royalty in my blood. And Ky had his sights set on me. It was daunting."

"My best friend acts like Solomon is a vampire prince. I don't get it. He's just a paranormal like the rest of us. There is no vampire royalty."

"Have you met his parents yet?"

"His mom but not his dad." Raven quirks her eyebrow in question. "She wasn't terrible. We didn't become besties or anything. She made me see something about myself I didn't want to face."

"I think you got off lucky, because Eloise Verascue is a force to be reckoned with. Do you know that no one can teleport here? Ky had this place made so it's not possible. Yet one night, Seth and Eloise popped in and didn't care what Ky and I were doing. They teleported here—a place no other paranormal can. The power those two have is immense. There're also no boundaries with that female."

"Sounds about right," I mutter. I remember what she said to Ford in the bar about wanting grandchildren.

"Back to what we were talking about. You're Sol's mate, yes?" I nod. "But you're not mated yet?" I shake my head. "What's holding you back?" It feels odd to be spilling my guts to someone I don't know, but maybe that's best. She has no reference point for me. She doesn't know me at all. She can give an unbiased opinion.

"My mom died giving birth to me and my dad gave me away when I was four."

Raven gasps and brings her hand to her mouth. "I'm so sorry. That must have been awful." I shrug, trying to act like it wasn't so bad, when in reality there's a part of my heart I don't think will ever heal.

"I never knew my mom and I was four when I went to stay with Vanessa." I push on before she can say anything, needing to get out what I want to say. "I've always been very independent, not relying on anyone except the mage who took me in, and my best friend, who's a bear shifter. It's easier not to get hurt when there's no one who can break your heart. I stayed away from males, not wanting a mate. I was so young when my dad left, but I remember with clarity the pain he was in when he looked at me. I reminded him of his dead mate." I shake my head. "I can't imagine that kind of pain. But he ran like a coward and couldn't be bothered to raise me like a decent male."

"You've been through a lot in a short time. Sol said we're close in age. To lose both parents…" She shakes her head with sympathy in her eyes.

"It wasn't a walk in the park, knowing I wasn't wanted or loved by my dad, but I think I did okay. I'm a powerful paranormal who can take care of herself."

She nods. "How did you meet Solomon?" I smile. I can't help myself. Yes, he's a huge pain in my butt. However, I remember how he got under my skin more than any other male right from the start.

I tell Raven about our encounters and how he slowly wore me down. I tell her about the explosion and how we're not sure if someone is after Donovon, Tristin, or me. She listens raptly and only speaks now and then; absorbing the information I'm giving her. I try to step outside my head and look at things from her point of view. Does she see me as a rebellious child or someone who's fighting through life, trying to make the best of it? Or does she care about Sol and want to be protective of him?

"What if we mate and then he leaves me?" I ask, voicing my fears. "What if he realizes I'm not enough for him? I'm literally no one, Raven. I live in a tiny apartment and have minimal money."

"Fortunately, Sol doesn't need to be fed often." She winks at the corny joke and I groan. Of course, he needs to eat more than human food. Why didn't I think about that before?

"He's going to want to suck on my neck," I state,

groaning again. "He's going to want to drink my blood."

"Yeah, he is," she says in a suggestive tone, while smiling and nodding.

"For fate's sake. You're as bad as Sol. I can barely say anything without him making it dirty."

"Sorry. I couldn't help myself."

I wave her off. "It's fine. I'm just moody."

"That's understandable. There's a lot going on in your head right now between the whole someone trying to kill you and being Sol's mate. What I can tell you is that from what I've seen, and what I've heard, Sol doesn't want casual. He's been lonely for a long time, filling his bed with casual hook-ups."

I grimace. "You're not making me feel any better." I don't want to think about Sol with other females in his bed, let alone a revolving door of them.

"Sorry. I'm not saying this right. Think of Sol as a dog at a shelter. Day after day goes by and there are friendly people who come in and walk past his run. Some let him out and he gets to play with them and lick their face, but eventually he's put back in and passed over for a different dog. No matter who Sol's met, he's never found someone for himself. So, he sits at home and glances out at the ocean, wondering when it's going to be his turn. Because, like that dog at the shelter, when he does find his home, and that's what you'll be to him by the way—home—he'll be the most loyal companion you'll ever have." I probably wouldn't have used that analogy, but I get what she's trying to say.

To think of Sol alone, with no one special, makes my chest hurt. Sure, he's been intimate with females, but if they never shared a connection with him then every encounter probably left him empty.

"You don't think he'll leave?" I ask, my voice laced

with uncertainty and a little bit of hope.

Raven reaches over and lays her hand on mine, careful to shield her emotions as I do the same. "I haven't known that male for centuries or even a decade, but well enough that if he's your mate, he'll prove his love for you every day of his life. That's what these males do. There is no in-between with them. When they leap, when they love, they do so with their entire being." Something inside of me settles at her words. A sort of peace falls over me. Can it be that simple? All I have to do is open myself up to him, accept our mate bond, and I'll have him forever?

"If we're close in age, how did you get so smart? I feel like I'm light-years behind you."

"Spend some time with the royal family and you'll learn how to take a step back and watch everything around you. It's not so bad being an observer sometimes. Also, being with Ky is like having a tour guide as a mate. We've traveled all over the mortal realm, gone to many other realms. I've seen a lot. Once you put it into perspective and really look at the one by your side, you realize there is no one else you'd rather experience life with. Sol is that for you. You just have to give him a chance. He won't take you for granted, Lilah. He won't break your heart. He's a good male. For all his quick wit, casual words, and air of recklessness, buried deep inside is a male who wants nothing more than to be loved."

# Chapter Seventeen

*Solomon*

**"YOU NEED TO GO** GET MY FEMALE and bring her back," I seethe to Kylest. "Better yet, portal me there."

Kylest sits on my sofa as if he doesn't have a care in the world. As if I'm not about to lunge for him and make him pay for not bringing me to my female. "You forget who you're talking to," he says casually.

"The same can be said to you."

"I'd say that would be an interesting fight, but I don't need to move to kill you, so you wouldn't stand a chance." He's right. We both know it. I still want to strangle him, though.

Instead, I flop down on the couch next to him in a huff. "Why couldn't they talk here?"

"Going somewhere else gave them much-needed space. Besides, Raven won't let anything happen to Lilah. And the only ones who can enter my home in the in-between are my family and your parents."

"We saw how loyal your family was."

Ky turns and gives me a death glare. "Low blow, Solomon. Watch yourself."

"I'm sorry. I just want her back."

He nods. "I can understand that."

They could have talked here. Kylest or Raven could have used their magic so we didn't hear anything. They would have had privacy. But no, they had to go to the in-between. I do trust Kylest and Raven with my life. However, this isn't my life we're talking about. It's Lilah's.

We sit in silence for a bit. There's nothing I want to talk to him about. Not when all I can think about is Lilah. I wonder what Raven is telling her. Will she want to mate with me when she gets back and we're alone again? Blood races through my body at the thought. I'd love to taste her while bringing us together.

"You need to feed, Sol."

"I know." I scrub a hand over my face as my stomach rumbles. "She's the only one I want. No other human or vampire is good enough to munch on."

"Your words are so elegant. It's amazing you don't have females throwing themselves at your feet," he deadpans.

I smile. "I do. Just not the one I want."

"That's the reason she's your mate. She challenges you. Can you imagine what it would be like if you had someone for your mate that let you walk all over them, do what you want, and only there to serve you?"

I grin. "Serve me, huh? I could get used to that."

"You're such a child."

I snort. "Like I haven't heard that before."

Kylest chuckles. "It is fun spending time with you. There aren't many I can relax around and laugh."

"I aim to please, Kylest."

"Call me Ky." I quirk an eyebrow. The fae has a nickname.

"I like it. Not so fancy and formal. It's like you're one of us lowly peasants."

"You're hardly lowly, Sol."

"I'm no prince." He laughs.

We talk a little while longer. I try not to wonder if Lilah and Raven are still in the in-between and how long they've been gone. So much could happen to them, but Ky's right. Raven has his powers now, so she's strong. And they aren't out in the open somewhere. At least, not that I'm aware of.

Then all of a sudden I hear a noise. Followed by another one. It's close but not in the room. I barely have to time to register that it's the sound of a pin being pulled from a grenade and a thud before the front wall of my house blows apart, throwing Kylest and me across the room.

As soon as we land, Ky is up on his feet. He's searching around us, his magic thick in the air. How did he move so fast? He's like some super paranormal. I'm still trying to get my bearings.

"Raven, get back!" Ky yells, alerting me to the fact that the females are now in the middle of this mess with us. Wow, my vampire skills are really rocking today.

"No way," Raven replies as the magic in the air hangs heavier.

I scramble to my feet and rush over to stand in front of Lilah. She shoves me aside. "I'm not helpless."

"No, but your well-being is the most important thing in the world to me."

She doesn't listen. Instead, she puts her back to mine so no one can sneak up on us. Raven does the same to Ky and we form a tight circle of death for anyone who comes near us.

We slowly step away from one another so we can cover a greater area. Each of us assesses our surroundings, trying to find the one who did this. Minutes tick by. There's no one. Whoever threw that did it and left quickly.

Sirens can be heard in the distance. Great. More cops to deal with. I quickly walk back over to the paranormals beside me. "You have to go. Take Lilah. I'll text you when to come get me. I have to talk to the cops and make up a story. I have natural gas in the house, so I can play it off that it was the cause of the explosion. At least for now. There's no way I can say someone lobbed a grenade at me."

"That's what caused this?" Lilah asks with wide eyes. "You could have been killed!"

Raven shivers and presses close to Kylest, who quickly opens a portal as the sirens close in. For a moment, Lilah hesitates, but she must see something in my eyes. Something that tells her I need to handle this. I don't want to worry about her while trying to convince the police of my story.

Lilah places her palm on my chest and presses a quick kiss to my lips. "Be safe. Come to me as soon as you're done."

I nod. "I vow it."

Within a few seconds, they're gone, and the portal closes as a sea of police cruisers with their lights flashing come up my driveway. The cops get out and rush over to me, asking if I'm okay, what happened, and so on.

Fortunately, I look like I've been blown across my house, which I have. My clothes are singed, I'm covered in grey dust, and I'm sure my hair has blood in it. I'm healed. Nothing hurts. But my head was cut when I landed.

Fire trucks and ambulances are the next to show up as one of the officers radios in about a potential gas leak, and I'm pulled from the house. I'm kept a safe distance away as he orders everyone else to get back.

****

Many hours later, I'm texting Ky to come pick me up in the woods behind my house in Jersey. I refused medical treatment repeatedly, assured them I had a place to stay, and promised not to go back into the home until the gas company did a thorough investigation. Like I'd listen to them. For now, the gas is shut off.

As soon as they were gone, I teleported upstairs and grabbed Lilah's belongings, knowing not only would she want her clothes but also the picture that is so important to her.

My stuff was thrown into my duffle bag, not paying mind to what I was grabbing. I could always buy more clothes. There's nothing with me of sentimental value. I learned long ago to travel light and keep everything disposable. The last thing I wanted was to be traveling and lose something of importance. Whatever I have with me is replaceable. Well, except for Lilah. She's more precious than any belongings.

As I wait for a response from Ky and a portal, I think back to the time since I've met Lilah. Yes, it's been for a very short period, but she's become everything to me. I guess that happens when lives are in danger and you realize what you stand to lose. It puts everything into perspective.

A shimmery silver portal opens up in front of me. Instead of Ky coming through, Lilah does. She's on me immediately, causing me to drop the bags I'm holding. Her arms wrap around my neck as she holds me tightly. I return the embrace, grateful she wasn't here when the grenade went off. No, it wouldn't have killed her, but the person or paranormal responsible would have used it as a diversion to get what they wanted. Maybe that's why we didn't find anyone. Because Lilah wasn't here. She wasn't inside. Yet they knew how to find us.

The only ones who knew where we were staying were Ford, Sienna, Ky, and Raven. None of them would tell anyone. Which leads me to believe that not only is this individual off the deep end crazy, but they know more about me than I'm comfortable with. No one knows about this house. I've never brought anyone here outside of my family. Yet, we were found.

"I hated leaving you," Lilah says, with her face tucked into my neck.

"I was safe."

Pulling back, she peers up at me. "You weren't, but if I stayed, I would have distracted you. Now, come on. I don't want to be here anymore." She glances around, her nerves apparent.

I take one last look at my home through the trees. Yellow crime scene tape surrounds it and there are bits of debris scattered around the yard. I'm going to have to find a contractor to come out here and give me a quote for the repairs. It's not like I have homeowner's insurance. I can afford to pay for whatever needs to be done while avoiding all the bull that comes along with filing a claim and waiting for work to get started.

Together, each holding a bag, we step through the portal. On the other side is Ky and Raven's home in the in-between.

Ky closes the portal upon our arrival and takes our bags. I watch as he puts them in a room to my back right. "You can stay here as long as you like. You're obviously not safe in the mortal realm. The fae realm would be too overwhelming for Lilah, if I had to guess. She might be one of us, but it's a lot to take in if you're not used to it."

"Thank you," she replies. "I've never been there. I'm

not sure if I ever want to go. But at least here we're safe. No one can follow us."

Ky nods. "I've used my magic to give you two privacy. When you're in the bedroom, we won't be able to hear anything you say." *"Or do,"* he says in my mind and winks. "Help yourself to food, whatever you need."

"Thank you," I tell him. "Unfortunately, hiding here won't solve the mystery of who's doing this. I need to get back out there tomorrow and put a stop to this. Is there a way you can do whatever to this place so I can teleport in and out?"

"Yes, I'll handle it in the morning. Until then, should you need to go somewhere, just ask Raven or me and we'll open a portal." Lilah can as well, but we wouldn't be able to portal back. Plus, I don't want her going with me when I leave. I'd rather have her here safe.

In the bedroom with the door closed, I strip off my ruined clothes and toss them into a small garbage can in the corner. They reek of smoke. When I turn around, Lilah is watching me from where she's perched on the bed.

"See something you like?" I ask and pivot, showing off my best side, which is my back side, obviously. You could bounce a quarter off my butt.

"You're very comfortable in your skin, aren't you?"

"Of course. I'm a powerful vampire and I'm hung like a—"

"Sol! I wasn't talking about that," she says and points her finger at my very impressive… package. Yeah, she likes what she sees. "I can hear you! Do you ever take a break from the dirty thoughts running through your head?" It seems I let my block down without even realizing it.

"I'm not doing it consciously. It comes to me as easily as the English language does. Second nature."

Lilah groans, throws herself back onto the bed, and puts her arm over her eyes. What I wouldn't give to cross the room and climb over her lithe body. But I don't because I smell bad and am covered in ash.

Turning, I leave the room to go to the bathroom. The living space is quiet. Ky and Raven must be in their bedroom. I take a quick shower, using the products they have. Leaning my head down, I sniff my wet arm. I smell like a garden of wisteria. If they're going to have guests over, they need to have more than this. There should be more manly stuff in here, too. Soap that smells like pine trees and musk.

The scent of the bodywash floats to me again. Okay, maybe the smell isn't so bad after all.

*Lilah*

**"I DON'T SUPPORT THIS," I STATE FIRMLY.**

"I don't care," Sol responds.

"You're seriously going back to Duck to look for whomever is after me?"

"I'm going to park my butt in my home and wait for someone to come. And when they do, I'll be ready." I can't believe he's doing this. He'll be a sitting duck… in Duck. And I'm supposed to stay here and act like it's fine that he's out there fighting battles for me? I don't think so.

"I'm coming with you."

"Absolutely not."

I put my hand on my hip. "Last time I checked, you don't tell me what to do."

"Lilah…"

"My name is Constance," I growl. Sure, I've totally accepted him calling me Lilah, but he's irritating me, and in turn, I'm doing the same to him. I'm not about his caveman behavior.

He shakes his head. "I'm not arguing with you anymore. I'm doing this whether you like it or not."

"Well, don't expect me to be waiting around for you when you get back."

His eyes widen and his mouth hangs open in a moment of shock. "You don't mean that."

"Test me." It's then I'm grateful Kylest put a barrier up around our room so they can't hear us, because I'd bet money they'd both have something to say.

Sol walks to me with that predatory gait of his and keeps coming until I'm pushed to the wall behind me, nowhere left to go. "You want me to test you? You want me to see how far I can push you?" I nod. "You asked for it."

Sol leans down and crushes his mouth to mine. At first, I don't yield to him even as the spark from our connection flares to life. I fight him until his tongue teases my lips and his hand lifts my shirt at my waist so he can trace his fingers along the skin on the small of my back. I can't help it. I cave.

I open my mouth and his tongue immediately searches for mine. I melt into him. There's no holding back. Not when my body is ablaze and my mind is drunk on everything to do with the male in front of me.

Reaching up, I thread my fingers into his hair, loving the silky feel of his locks. My nails rake over his scalp and Sol groans into my mouth. Then his hands smooth down my sides as his body dips so he can grasp the backs of my thighs. He lifts me in the air, and I instinctively wrap my legs around his waist. Within a few strides, we're on the bed, Sol over me.

Is this what I've been missing out on? Having a male to light every nerve ending in my body or is this just Sol?

"It's me, kitten," he says when his lips break from mine. "I've never felt this with another female."

"Tell me." I need to find out what's so special about

me. I don't want to be one of Sol's conquests. I want to be everything to him. The only one who drives him crazy with need. The only one who will ever share his bed again.

That thought slams into me like a wrecking ball. I'm done trying to work this out. I want all of him. No other female will ever again touch what's mine.

"All I have to do is look at you, Lilah, and my body awakens. Your scent, your voice, the way you walk, it drives me wild. And when you touch me—that touch I've been waiting for since I met you—desire races through my body and all I can think of is you. You have more power in your finger than anyone else when it comes to me."

Emotion clogs my throat. "Sol…"

"Say you want me, Lilah. Tell me I can taste your skin and drink from you. Tell me I can make you mine once and for all."

"Yes," I purr as my cat rises to the surface and my body arches into his, needing his weight on me. Needing him to take me away for a bit. I want this connection with him.

"Kitten, you're the only female I will ever want for the rest of my life."

I'm about to respond when he dips his head and drags his fangs along the column of my neck. A shiver races up my spine in anticipation. He's going to bite me, and I want it. I want to be the one who sustains his life.

Gripping his head in my hands, I pull him back until our eyes meet. "Promise me you'll only drink from me from now on. I don't want you seeking out any other female for blood."

"I vow it."

I tilt my head to the side, exposing my neck for him. "Bite me, Solomon Verascue."

He smiles this wicked, deviant smile. "With pleasure."

He's there again; fangs out over my skin. I tense for a moment, then he pierces me. The sting of the bite isn't bad. It's quickly followed by a level of bliss I never knew existed. I'm not just soaring; I'm on a whole other plane.

He takes a long pull of my blood and writhes against me. I don't bother trying to remove his clothes with my hands; I use my magic and rid him of everything with one flick of my wrist. I do the same to myself. The second our bare skin touches, we both moan in pleasure. His hands move over my skin, driving me higher.

"Please, Sol," I beg. I need him. Now. Every part of my being, including my cheetah, calls out for him to make us his.

Sol moves above me and within moments, we're joined as he continues to drink from me.

I expect bliss but what I get is so much more. Our hearts beat in tandem. Our minds meld and our thoughts, memories, everything floats to the other. We didn't bond over time like a shifter pair. No, we bond all at once and it's glorious.

Something else hits me—a raw surge of power. I have no doubt Solomon is gifting me something through his bite. I honestly don't even care what it is. I want everything he has to give me. This male is mine for the rest of eternity, and if I'm going to be his equal in every way, I'll take his power. I want to be there for him as he will be for me.

Three words float from his mind to mine as he takes another pull of my blood. *"I love you."*

Tears immediately pool in my eyes as a wave of emotion crashes over me. How can this male, who barely knows me, feel so strongly so fast? Wetness on my cheeks tells me I wasn't able to keep the tears at bay, but as quickly as they came, they're pushed away as Sol continues to move.

I'm drunk on his love and the pleasure he's giving me.

Higher and higher he pushes us until we crash together in a symphony of rapid heartbeats, fast breaths, sweaty limbs, and the solid feeling of rightness. Nothing in my life has ever felt as perfect as this moment.

I cry out his name and hold my legs around his waist tightly, never wanting to let go.

Sol retracts his fangs from my neck and seals the wound with his tongue. I don't have to shift to replenish my blood loss. My fae side will take care of it and heal my body.

Lifting his head, Sol's gorgeous grey eyes peer down at me. So much emotion is there. So many different feelings I can't begin to process. "I meant what I said. I love you, Lilah. Don't pick it apart or wonder how I can so quickly. I know my heart, and it's only beat for you since I first walked into that bar. I surrender to you. You own every part of me."

"What will others say?"

"Screw everyone else. I have never cared what people thought of me and I'm sure not going to start now. None of them matter. Only you. Only us."

"It's easy to say that, but your family means the world to you. I have your thoughts now, Sol. You can't hide from me." Going through all his memories, his thoughts, it's going to take me a while to grasp everything I now know about Solomon Verascue.

"I never tried to."

A slight burning of my wrist causes my gaze to snap to it. The inside of my left wrist now bears two small red dots, as if he'd bitten me there.

"I'm marked," I murmur as I hold up my wrist so he can see it.

He cradles my arm in his hand and presses a chaste kiss to the spot. "Forever," he whispers.

I can't believe we did it. Not just the physical act, but we're mated. I have someone who will always be in my life. As quick as those feelings arrive, so does the one of dread. The sheer fear that he will leave me one day.

He cups my cheek in his hand, no doubt hearing my thoughts, and draws my gaze to his. "Never. I won't ever abandon you. I will always be there for you, no matter what." There's something freeing about him having access to my thoughts. Not that he didn't before, however, he never crossed the line between us. There's no more hiding for me. No more running.

Sol rolls to his side and brings me with him. The stupid smile on his face has me grinning as well. "Best make-up sex ever."

"You had to say it, didn't you?"

"You not only get to listen to my mouth for the rest of your life, but you also get a backstage pass to every dirty thought I'll ever have."

"It's like a porno you can't shut off."

"You have no idea."

I smack him lightly on the chest. "Just wait until you hear my thoughts at night when I come home after working at the bar."

His eyes darken. "You're not going to work there anymore. You're a Verascue now. You'll never want for anything."

"Rein it in, Sol. I don't need you clubbing me over the head and dragging me to your den of sin. I'm still the same independent woman I was when you met me."

"Fine. If you insist on working there, then I'll go with you every time."

My mouth drops open. "No way. You can't do that."

"I can and I will. Don won't throw me out. He likes me. I read it in his mind."

I groan and put my hand over my eyes. "What did I get myself into?"

"You didn't get into anything, but I got into y—"

I slap my hand over his mouth. "Don't finish that sentence." He chuckles behind my palm. "Being mated to you is going to be like having a teenager around all the time, isn't it?"

"In my mind, yes, but the rest of me is one-hundred-percent sinful vampire who has experience and amazing rebound abilities."

"You're terrible."

He sits back and stares openly at me. His gaze sweeps down my naked body and back up again. "You need clothes on before I introduce you to Kylest and Raven as my mate."

"I don't need an introduction. I already know them."

"Yes, you do. You're mine now. Everyone will know it," he says with an air of authority. Slowly, he trails his palm from my ankle, up my leg, to my hip, to my side, then my shoulder. "Dress yourself with magic, kitten. Something I'll love." I flick my wrist to put clothes on and Sol immediately pulls back and scrunches up his nose. "What did you do?"

"What?" I ask innocently. "You don't like this?" I put myself in a heavy parka, snow pants, gloves, and a thick hat. The least sexy outfit I could think of.

"You did that on purpose! I can't admire you when you look like you're going sledding."

"I'm sorry." I'm absolutely not. "Not to your liking?"

He leans over me and presses the length of his hard, still naked body to mine. All thought of pushing him away flees. "Dress for me, Lilah," he whispers in my ear before taking it between his teeth.

I immediately do as he asks and change my outfit to something more appropriate—a pair of blush-colored shorts and a white tank top with a lacy edge. “Better?”

“Much.” Sol traces along the edge of the tank top with his finger then meets my gaze. “Round two is about to start.”

I laugh and reach up to pull him down to me so I can kiss him again. I’ll have to deal with his dirty sense of humor for the rest of my life, but there’s no doubt in my mind that I made the right call in mating with him. Now to get rid of whoever is trying to kill us so Sol and I can live happily ever after.

# CHAPTER NINETEEN

*Solomon*

**WITH LILAH'S HAND** IN MINE, MY POWER flowing through her veins, and her blood coursing through mine, we step out of the room a newly mated couple.

It's the next morning. I wanted to introduce us as mated last night, but I ended up never getting out of bed and devoured Lilah all night long. So this morning it is.

Raven is at the stove cooking and Ky is sitting at the table watching his mate. Per usual, they're dressed similarly in black pants and olive green shirts. Ky's hair is a deep red while Raven's is her natural midnight black with red tips to match Ky. They both turn as we enter and smile wide.

"You're finally mated," Ky says and stands. He hugs me. I'm stunned for a moment then hug him back. He doesn't normally embrace me. Paige, Ari, sure. Not me. He doesn't hug Lilah, though. Maybe it's because we're newly mated and my possessive side is at the level of a billion. Raven, however, goes over and hugs her.

"I'm so happy for you both," she says. "Come sit down. Breakfast is almost done." The scent of sausage is strong in the air, and I don't mean that in the dirty sense.

"Thank you for cooking," I say. I have a strong appetite. Especially after spending the night ravaging my mate.

My mate. It's going to take me a bit to get used to it. I can't help but smile like a lovesick fool at the thought of it. I finally have someone who's mine. No one will be connected to her like I am. And I will never again have an empty bed.

*"What makes you think I'm going to sleep in your bed every night?"* Lilah asks in my head.

I swing my gaze to her. I have to get used to her having free access to my head. *"You will never sleep away from me. Not as long as my heart beats. I will always be with you."*

*"Then I'm going with you today when you head home. I'm not staying behind while you search for whoever attacked us."* Clever female.

*"I can't risk your safety."*

*"You forget that I'm a cheetah, fae, and also have your powers. Whichever you gave me."*

*"All. I gave you everything."*

*"Good. I could slit any threat's throat with a flick of my wrist or sever their head with my bare hands and sit back while you drain their body."*

*"Is it wrong that I'm completely turned on at the thought of that?"* The fantasy takes hold in my mind. Lilah cutting down paranormal after paranormal. She's going to be a force to be reckoned with.

I can't keep her hidden away, though, as much as I want to. She can teleport now. I just have to teach her how. That's way easier than opening a portal. I'd have to put magical handcuffs on her to keep her still. Hey, that's not a bad idea. I could cuff her to a bed. Have her waiting for me when I return.

*"If you think I won't murder you where you stand if you ever do that to me, you mated the wrong female."*

*"I love it when your claws come out."*

Ky clears his throat. "Would you two like us to leave?"

I turn to him. "What? Why?"

"I'm waiting for you to drag her on top of the table and put on a show for us. Not that we'd be opposed to watching, but that's kind of a private thing."

I look back at Lilah and realize we're only inches apart. Her hand fists the front of my shirt and we're leaning over the table toward one another, inches apart. When did that happen?

"I think we need to learn some self-control around others, kitten. I'd rather not let anyone see every inch of your delectable body."

She snaps out of the lust-filled haze and glances around before releasing me and leaning back. "Good call." At least I'm not the only one affected.

We eat breakfast and talk. I resist every urge to drag Lilah back to the bedroom and strip her bare. Too bad I didn't get her fae magic when we mated. Only fae royals share their magic with their mates.

After we eat and thank them profusely for bringing us to their home, we gather our bags and Ky tells me I can teleport in and out of his home in the in-between. But it's with a warning to text Raven first, unless it's an emergency. He doesn't want me interrupting anything between them.

When we land in my home, not one sound is heard. It's eerie.

Then twenty or so paranormals pop out from every possible place and yell "Congrats!" I jump about ten feet in the air as my fangs descend, ready to kill everyone. Only it's my friends and family. They're lucky to still have their heads.

"Why would you do that?" I yell at my brother and Wake, who are standing side by side.

"You do remember what you did to Paige and me when we mated, right?" Wake asks. I couldn't forget it. I had a banner hung to welcome the new couple.

"I hate you," I mutter. He had to get me back, didn't he?

"You love me." He slings his arm over my shoulders as my fangs retract and brings me in for a hug. "You're one of us now, Sol. We can go on double dates. You and Lilah can watch the girls for us. We can vacation together. It's going to be so much fun."

"You've lost your mind."

"No way, bestie. Welcome to the world of responsibility."

"You take that back! I'm not ready to be responsible."

"You're fifteen hundred years old," he states. "It's about time you grow up."

Lilah's laugh breaks through our conversation, drawing my attention to her. All I see is my mate laughing with someone with jet-black hair pulled up into a ponytail. I know immediately who it is and can only imagine the things she's telling my female. I don't bother to excuse myself from the conversation with Wake. I walk right over and put myself between Ariane and Lilah.

"What's so funny?"

"I was telling Lilah about the time you hit on another vampire and she shot you down." Ari chuckles. "I hadn't seen that happen up until that point. It was fantastic." I narrow my gaze at her, but she doesn't give me a chance to talk. "Oh, and about the time I showed up at your home to find you watching a romantic movie and crying. Classic."

"You're evil!"

"Yes, yes, I am. This isn't news to you, Sol. You're lucky I don't drag Merrick and Zayda down here to pick on you, too." Ari's aunt and uncle are both wolf shifters. Merrick is the alpha of a pack up in Pennsylvania. One I used to drop in on from time to time to drive the wolves crazy. It was so easy to work them up and I was bored.

"I can handle them."

She scoffs. "Sure you can."

"Solomon, are you going to properly introduce us to your mate?" My mother's formal tone pulls me back to reality and away from the conversation with Ari. She smirks and spins in search of her mate who isn't far from her. Traitor. Ari could have stayed and been a buffer.

"I've only been here for a few minutes, Mother. I haven't had the chance to make my way around the room." Taking Lilah's hand in mine, we both face one of the most intimidating couples in the universe. "Mother, Father, this is my mate, Lilah. I hope you'll treat her like family."

"Watch what you wish for, son," my dad says. Seth Verascue is scary in his own right. But his appearance doesn't make you want to shrink back like my mom's does.

Dad is dressed in a pair of khaki shorts, tan boat shoes, and a hunter green polo shirt. His blond hair is combed back from his face and the warm smile he's wearing has Lilah relaxing a little beside me.

"Lilah, it's lovely to meet you," he says with a dip of his head. He's careful to respect her fae side.

My mom, on the other hand, decides to walk around Lilah in a slow circle to take her in. "I remember you from the bar and liked your personality. You don't like me much and that's okay. You're smart to be reserved." Mom stops in front of Lilah, her eyes holding those of my mate. Her slim jeans tight and her white, sleeveless blouse is tucked into them. She's easily got fifty grand of diamonds dripping from her neck and ears.

"Are you done?" Lilah asks, her voice firm. A hush falls over those near us so they can listen to what my mom will say next. Not many talk back to her. Ford, Dad, me, sure. But Lilah is new to the family.

"Am I done what? Assessing you? Seeing if you're a worthy female for my son? I'm not sure."

"I'm sorry. I forgot the part where I was supposed to ask for your permission. Your son and I are mated. I didn't choose him. Fate did. Like it or not, I'm part of your family. We can be cordial to one another or try to think of ways to kill each other every time we're in the same room. The choice is yours." Holy fate. I don't think I've ever heard anyone talk to my mom that way and live.

"Uh, kitten, maybe now would be a good time to get a drink," I tell her with a gentle tug of her hand.

"No, Sol. Don't take her anywhere. You're not scared of me, are you?" she asks Lilah.

"No. There aren't many in this world I'm truly afraid of. I've learned that showing fear is a sign of weakness, and I'm not a timid female."

Mom looks her up and down. "You need nicer heels." Lilah put on a short-sleeved shirt and a pair of very short shorts after breakfast, along with her black heels I love so much. "Once this is sorted out with whomever blew up my son's home, and tried to kill you both, I want you to come to Italy and go shopping with me. There's a man who makes custom shoes. You need a pair of heels worthy of your stature."

"And what stature is that?" Lilah inquires with her head held high.

"You're a Verascue now, dear. You're going to represent our family. In doing so, you're going to wear the best shoes money can buy." Mom leans in close. "Also, there's going to be a sharp blade hidden in the heel. You never know when you'll need it." She winks. My mom freaking winks.

A portal opens and Ky and Raven step out, distracting my parents from the conversation we're having. They immediately go over to the fae couple to talk. I have no doubt it was Ky who tipped my brother off to Lilah and me becoming mates. Or Raven. It was one of them. No one else knew. We weren't even in the same realm.

Ford sidles up next to me. "What just happened?"

We both stare at Lilah. "I think Mother met her match," I reply.

"We should've recorded this. We're likely never to see it again."

Lilah rolls her eyes. "You two are idiots. She's a female just like me. I wasn't about to stand here and let her talk to me like that or tell me all the reasons why I don't belong in this family. Screw that."

Sienna comes over and hugs Lilah tightly, catching her by surprise. Lilah lets out a yelp but is careful to keep their skin from touching. "I wasn't sure whether to hug you or hide," Sienna admits. "I was seriously waiting for her to rip you apart in front of everyone. Not kill you but cut you down with her words. I can't believe you did that. I wish I had the kind of courage you do." My brother's mate has come a long way since they first reconnected, but she's never been a tough female.

"I'm immortal" Lilah replies. "The last thing I want is Sol's mother thinking she can talk down to me for the rest of my life. Nope. Not gonna happen."

I tug Lilah toward me and press my lips to hers. "You're amazing," I say against them. Then in her mind I ask, *"What do you say we get out of here and I show you just how perfect I think you are?"*

*"We're in the middle of a celebration. I think they'd realize if the guests of honor leave."*

*"Ten minutes. That's all I need."*

She pulls back to look into my eyes. *"If you're trying to sell me on this idea, saying it's only going to last ten minutes isn't the way to do it."* Feisty cheetah.

*"I love you."* I grin.

*Lilah*

**AFTER THE PARTY WINDS** DOWN AND EVERYONE portals or teleports home, Sol has a talk with his brother about having a party when we've been under attack. Talk might not be the right word. Sol shoved him against the wall, and the two went at it for a while until they both got sick of fighting and went to their separate corners of the house.

I understand Sol's frustration, but his brother would never put him in danger. Plus, with the sheer power of everyone in the house, even the smartest person or paranormal would have been a fool to attack here.

The day is over and we're exhausted. I want to go to sleep, but Sol's on edge.

"We can't stay here," he says while yawning.

"We have to stay somewhere. We're in no shape to look for anyone tonight."

"I have an idea."

Ford stands and comes over, stopping in front of us. "Tell me where you're going. I can't help if I don't know where you are. It was bad enough your house blew up in

Jersey and I wasn't there."

Sol ignores the comment about Ford not being there. He wouldn't have wanted him in harm's way. "I can't give away all my secrets."

"We shouldn't have any, brother." There's something in Ford's eyes that causes Sol to buckle. He has homes no one else is aware of and he does for a reason. But maybe he can start letting people in again. He puts on this couldn't care less front when those who are closest to him understand how truly false it is.

Sol chooses to send the location to Ford via telepathy. It's smart. There could be someone outside listening, though Kylest did say he put up a shield around Sol's and Ford's homes so no one could hear what goes on. That doesn't mean the home is impenetrable. A bomb could blow the house apart.

Sol finishes talking to Ford then takes my hand in his.

"Thank you for this tonight," I say to Ford. "While it was unexpected, and not something I would have ever wanted to be done just because we're mated, I had a good time."

Ford smiles. "Keep your guard up. Sol's had many years of tormenting others. While this might be the first bit of revenge, I highly doubt it's the last." We still aren't sure who's being targeted, but it's clear it's not Don or Tris. That leaves Sol or me.

I shake my head. There's no doubt in my mind that Sol has gone around and screwed with a lot of people. If I didn't know better, I'd think there's a little fae in him.

His eyes pierce mine. *"No fae in me, kitten. But if you play your cards right, I'll be in a fae real soon."*

"Honestly!" I shout. "Does your brain ever shut off?"

Ford cocks his head then bursts out laughing. "I really

love you two together. You might like to give my brother grief, but you'll always laugh, Lilah."

"Yeah." I roll my eyes. "I can't wait until we're having a serious conversation, and he makes a remark about how good I'd look with my legs wrapped around him."

"Your legs are stunning," Sol interjects.

"Can we go?" I ask. "This is exhausting."

"It's only day one," he smirks. Sweet fate. I feel like I've been with him for a year.

Sol smiles before snapping his fingers, teleporting us and our bags to another location. When we land, I take a look around. Even with the darkened sky outside and the lights off, I can see clearly, thanks to my shifter night vision.

We're in a condo if I have to guess by the high location and open floor plan.

Sol steps away from me to flip on the lights then uses a remote to close the shades. They slip down over the wall of windows to conceal us. Everything is white. White walls, white furniture. I decide to walk around the space. The kitchen is white. Shock. At least the appliances are stainless steel. There are four bedrooms and four bathrooms. There is some color but not much. One bedroom has slate grey walls that match the en suite, which has grey flooring and a tile surround in the shower. Another room is beige. The next is an off white. And the biggest one, the master, is a steel color. Not shimmery silver but muted.

"Who decorated this place?" I ask. "There's no color. I'm going to wake up in the middle of the night and think I'm in some screwed up dream. You need to paint."

"You can decorate it if you want. What's mine is yours. Paint the whole thing red for all I care."

I turn to look at him and watch as he propels himself backward on the bed. "You must have chosen these colors for a reason."

"I like things clean and simple. But when I'm with you, everything seems to be magnified, intensified, and full of life. Maybe that's what I've been missing. You bring the whole color spectrum to my world."

Walking to the window, I move the shade aside and get my first real look at the view of the ocean. We could be anywhere, but I have a feeling we're still in the United States.

"You'd be right," he says, hearing my thoughts. "We're in Naples, Florida to be precise."

"You like the ocean, don't you?" I ask as I toe off my heels and walk over to lie beside him on the bed.

He reaches for my waist and pulls me in close until my head rests under his chin and my arms encircle him to hold him tightly. He smells so good. And lying here like this, I never knew I could need this comfort before. I always thought I was good on my own, when in reality, I was missing out on so much. This closeness, there's nothing like it. Solomon is mine. I'm the only one he'll hold like this for the rest of his life. Every part of me relaxes into him at the thought.

"The ocean is peaceful," he murmurs, bringing me back to the present. "It doesn't ask for anything from anybody. It's powerful and unyielding. But the sounds it makes, the way it can lull me to sleep when I'm on a boat, or sleeping in my home with the windows open, I could live like that the rest of my life. Salty air, sea birds flying overhead, dolphins playing not too far from shore, it's perfect. And now that I have you, I can experience it with new eyes. Because the sea isn't the only thing that brings me peace anymore. It's you, Lilah. You settle the darkest parts of my soul."

I melt at his words. For someone so incredibly tough and strong, Sol has this deep side of himself that I love seeing.

We lie there wrapped in each other for hours, talking, laughing, loving. Sleep eventually tries to claim us, though we both seem to be fighting it, not wanting to give up a moment of time we have together. You'd think for two paranormals who will live forever, barring an unfortunate beheading or silver stake in Sol's case, we'd sleep. We have many years ahead of us. However, we want to cherish every moment.

****

I'd like to say the morning sun coming through the cracks between the window and drawn shade is what wakes us the next morning. But I'd be wrong. It's a vampire. A yelling vampire. Saying something about an explosion.

Sol and I bolt upright and stare at Ford, whose hair is standing up as soot mars his chiseled jaw. Sienna stands by his side, her hand in his. She's frightened with wide eyes.

"If you don't figure out who this is soon, I'm going to murder whoever comes near me that I don't recognize! I won't even ask any questions. They take a wrong step and they're dead." Ford's tone is hard and unyielding. "I can't have someone setting off explosives near my mate. Your deck is gone, brother. The one facing the road. Obliterated."

"You think I want that?" Sol yells, throwing the blanket back and jumping from bed. "I can't figure out who's after Lilah or me. And now you're telling me I have no back deck. That's just lovely." My thoughts are jumbled, trying to keep up with the conversation. The brothers don't take a break; just keep talking.

"We could have been killed and you're worried about

your deck?"

Sol gets in Ford's face. "If you think for one second I'm more worried about my deck than I am about my own blood, you don't know me at all. But you're here, Ford—you and your mate. Do I like the idea that someone could have killed you? Absolutely not. But there's nothing I can do about the past. My goal was and is finding who's responsible and murdering them."

"Okay, I'll let that slide. I get it. I wasn't there in Jersey when you were." Ford scrubs a hand over his face before his eyes settle on me. "There's no one you can think of who'd want to do this to you, Lilah?"

"I don't have many friends," I say. I'm so tired of this. I want whoever this is caught and dealt with so we can all rest. "The only person who ever hated me is my father, and I don't have a clue where he is. He had the chance to kill me many years ago. I doubt he'd wait until now to do it. If he wanted me dead, he'd have killed me himself, instead of leaving me for someone else to raise." I didn't mean to let that out. Whatever.

"You have a point," Ford mumbles.

I stand and use my magic to change out of my pajamas and into a pair of black shorts that hit mid-thigh, a pastel pink tank top, and my killer heels. I'm done playing games. I have my original powers, plus Sol's. I can teleport. He told me how last night, but I haven't practiced yet. Can't be that hard. I've seen inside his head when he does it.

With that in mind, I picture the place I want to go to and snap. I'll deal with Sol's wrath later. Besides, I'm sure he knows how to find me. We're probably connected in that freaky shifter way where we can sense where our mates are.

I walk toward the taped off section of the bar and duck under the yellow plastic ringing the area. The bar isn't fixed and won't be for a while. It's going to take some work to get it back to where it was. I'm not skilled enough in my magic to wave a hand and fix it. Besides, what would we tell the humans when they see the bar rebuilt overnight? Some things have to be done conventionally.

My shoes crunch on broken glass as I make my way through the place, which became my second home. Every day that it sits like this, Don loses money. Luckily, he doesn't need it to survive. Being an older shifter has its perks. Like a surplus of money. Don loves to work, and I can't begin to imagine what he's going through not having the bar standing. This place means so much to him.

"Is there a reason you decided to leave me behind?" Sol hisses in anger at my back.

I feel so defeated at the moment. No, no one lost their life, but this bar, Don, Ford, and Sol, Tris for that matter, no one deserves to have their life screwed with, especially while Don is back home spending time with his family before he loses his father. He shouldn't have to worry about things here. I guess now he doesn't. There's no rush to fix it. At least not until he gets back.

"I can't sit around, Sol. You can't either. We need a plan to catch whoever did this so we can rebuild and stop putting your family at risk. I saw how upset Ford was. This has to end."

Turning, I watch as he rakes a hand through his hair. "I know, but you can't just leave like that, Lilah. I had to learn from Ford how to use my new instinct to tell me where you were. At least I have it. Who knew what we'd have since I'm a vampire and you're fae and a shifter. It's a pretty cool skill, by the way. Like a built-in compass, always pointing to you."

I offer him a small smile. "There are some perks to

being mated. I'm still learning all of them."

He steps close to me, kicking a few fallen bricks with his black boots as he does so. My eyes rake him over from his boots to his head. Dark jeans that fit perfectly. A black T-shirt, which hugs his arms and chest. "One of them is knowing you never have to do things on your own. Wherever you go, so will I. Don't leave me again. You scared me." For the first time, I can feel his emotions. The worry he had when I left. It hits me in the center of my chest, causing me to rub the spot there.

"Ford told me some things don't happen all at once," he says. "That sometimes it takes a bit for them to click into place." He takes my hand and brings it to his chest in the same spot. "I feel you there, too. I feel the love you have for me and how much you yearn for my touch." He embraces me. "Promise me you won't pull a stunt like that again." Love. I haven't said the words to him yet. That doesn't mean I don't feel them. Speaking them aloud… That's a whole other ball game.

I nod, hating the vulnerability in this tough vampire's voice. "I promise."

"Okay, now let's figure out what to do next.

# CHAPTER TWENTY-ONE

## *Solomon*

**IT'S BEEN A WEEK SINCE** SOMEONE BLEW APART my back deck. A week of sleeping in my home in Duck. A week of absolutely nothing. I can't figure out what this person or paranormal wants from us. I'm completely baffled.

I've thought about it long and hard. I don't think Lilah's dad would do this. If he wanted her dead, he's had her whole life to do so. So he's out. But who then?

We've gone to the bar numerous times, always at night so we're not seen. We've sifted through the rubble, looking for clues, and haven't found anything. The construction crew is set to start in a few days, and we wanted to make sure nothing was overlooked.

Tris even came to help us. If I didn't know him so well, and for so long, I'd consider him a suspect. But I can read his mind. There's nothing he can hide from me. He's completely innocent. And he's angry. A vampire with a temper is never a good thing. Tris has been simmering, waiting; hoping whoever did this shows, but nothing so far. He's taken to staying at my place. This way he can help. I don't think he likes being the third wheel with Lilah and me, but he's been my friend for a long time and wants to be here. I'll take that anytime.

Ford's been on edge and decided to move Sienna to the Avynwood Pack House a few days ago. She didn't want to go, but Paige shoved the twins at her and she melted. Ford's been going back and forth between here and the pack house. He's torn. On the one hand, he wants to protect his mate and always be at her side. On the other, family is very important to us and he wants to be here for us. I told him not to worry about us and take care of his mate, but he insists he can do both.

Then there are my parents. Seth and Eloise Versacue have been on a warpath. They have gone over each scene where there was an explosion, stayed at my house a few nights, gone to question Donovon. Nothing. It's like whoever is doing this is a ghost. Too bad ghosts aren't real, or I'd take it as a serious consideration.

We've reached the point where I'm just bored. We've traveled to Amalfi. Gone to Ford's house in Portland. I've shown Lilah every home I own. Or we own, rather. What's mine is hers and all that.

I can't go gallivanting around like I normally do since we still aren't sure where the threat is coming from. Everything is so up in the air while we wait for the next bomb to drop. It's grating on my last nerve.

"You need to stop pacing," Lilah says from her spot on the couch. I'm walking from the front of the home where it faces the ocean to the back where the new deck is already being built.

"I can't help it. I'm going out of my mind."

"He doesn't like staying in one place for too long," Ford says. "He gets stir crazy."

"Hey, I can stay in one spot just fine," I reply.

"Yes, if there's something going on. But there isn't and you're slowly losing it."

I snap my fingers and teleport upstairs to the master bedroom. There I pull open my top dresser drawer and retrieve my board shorts. Screw this. I'm going for a swim in the ocean.

Stepping out onto the upper deck, I lean over the white railing and take in the view. I never tire of seeing the ocean. In the distance is a tall sailboat. People play in the waves closer to shore. There's a lifeguard on duty. They don't say anything, but they're there. Always watching, scanning, waiting to rescue someone if need be.

I turn and lean against the railing as I look back into the house. The outside is a deep red with white trim. Red. Vampire. Yeah, I had to go there. The blue color it was when I moved in didn't cut it. The roof has a high peak over the deck where I stand. There are five bedrooms and four bathrooms up here and two more of each downstairs.

The open floor plan on the main level has a dining table that seats twelve, a massive sectional sofa that faces a gas fireplace with a television mounted above. The kitchen has white cabinets with a grey granite countertop and professional-grade, stainless steel appliances.

The home is bigger than Ford's, although I didn't care about that. All that mattered was living close to my brother.

"Going for a swim?" Lilah asks as she appears in the bedroom.

I shrug. "I don't know what else to do with myself."

"I'll come with you." With a quick burst of her magic, she replaces her clothes with a sapphire blue bikini. The bottom rests low on her hips, showing off her flat stomach. The top is strapless, covering only what's necessary. Something primal in me jumps to the surface as I cross the distance between us and pull her into my arms.

"Don't you have a one-piece you could put on? Maybe a big tunic over it?" I ask.

"Want to wear a shirt with your shorts?" she rebukes.

"Point taken."

I'm not putting on a shirt. Nope. No way. Her message is loud and clear. If I can go down there with my entire chest bare, she can wear a bikini. It's not like I'll have eyes on anyone but her. It's the humans I'll have to watch. I don't want anyone staring at what's mine.

"Ford is going to the pack house for a bit," she says. "Tris will hang out here until we get back."

I nod and take her hand in mine, teleporting us to the very lowest level of the home where we walk out to the pool area and up the stairs that lead us over the sand dune and onto the beach. I love having a private walkway. This way we don't have anyone else coming and going next to the house. The public access is about four houses to our left.

The beach is busy though not mobbed. Even in peak season, the only ones here are the ones living or renting nearby. There aren't any hotels around us, which I love. I don't like an overly crowded beach. That's not fun for anyone.

Down on the sand, we don't lay out a towel or set up chairs. I either want to be in the water swimming, helping others, or I'll stay on my deck at home and wait and listen.

Lilah and I walk hand in hand into the ocean. The water is warm and feels good against my skin. It's low tide, which means we can walk farther out, and the water only comes to our mid calves in spots. We keep going until we're waist-deep, then I wrap my arms around her and hold her close as the waves lift us with each passing one.

There's no rip current risk today, which is good. We

move farther out. There aren't many people where we are. A family in a large inflatable raft. A man on a paddleboard. Smaller kids are closer to shore with their parents.

"So, now that you have me out here, what are you going to do?" Lilah asks.

"If this weren't such a family-friendly area, I'd take you right here and now."

"Save that thought for later tonight when the beach is deserted. We can come back out, and you can make love to me in the ocean."

"Sweet fate, I love the way you talk." I crush my lips to hers, unable to resist the pull. I keep it from getting too heated, even though my body definitely wants to take it further.

We stay out there for an hour or so before walking back to shore. People are scattered about either on towels, in chairs, or under tents. Children dig holes and make sand castles.

Walking down the beach, we laugh and talk, all the while watching people as we go. I don't miss the hungry looks some of the males give Lilah. Nor does she miss the appreciative stares in my direction. I tighten my hand on hers, silently letting her know that she's it for me. As much as she's been trying to tamp down her jealous side, I see the death glare she gives other females. No matter how many times I tell her she's the only one I desire, she still has insecurities. I can't blame her. I do, too. It's hard to believe I get to have the gorgeous female by my side for all of eternity.

Something hits my leg, causing me to stop. I peer down and find a pair of sunglasses. Bending, I pick them up and notice they're not cheap ones. No, they have a designer name on the side. I glance around until my eyes land on a pair of eyes I'd recognize anywhere.

Mom and Dad are sitting in matching low-profile beach chairs. Mom has on a navy one-piece bathing suit, with a halter top and cut high over her hips. Dad's in a pair of grey board shorts, no shirt, leaving his chest and stomach on display. They look like a young, exceptionally fit couple, not the thousands of years old they are.

"Mother," I say. "These wouldn't be yours, would they?" I hold up the sunglasses.

"Why yes, they would. Do bring them to me." I walk over and bend down to hand them to her. "You really should watch where you're going, Solomon. You don't know who's out here, and you're oblivious to those around you."

I stand and defensively say, "I am not. I'm listening to everyone."

"Listening, yes. Watching, no. The very one after you and your mate could be out here as we speak, and you're so lost in your own world that they could be right under your nose."

"Got something you want to confess, female?" I ask, teasing her. She could be right, though. The one we seek could be out here, watching us.

"I'm always right," she replies, hearing my thoughts.

I open my mouth to reply, but my dad beats me to it. "Don't bother arguing. You've seen how she is. She's not going to change. And honestly, she only has your best interests at heart. If she didn't, we wouldn't be here." That brings up my next question.

"How long have you been here, exactly?"

"A week," Mom replies. "I do prefer Amalfi, but it's nice here. A few too many… people," she says, looking around. I have no doubt she would rather use the term humans.

"You don't have to stay. Ford is at my house, as is Tristin."

"I'm aware," Mom replies. "But the facts are that both of our children are here and there is a threat somewhere. I won't go far. I want to know if something happens." My parents will do whatever it takes to ensure Ford and I are always safe. Now that circle includes our mates.

"Where are you staying?" I ask. They could have stayed with Ford or me. Not that I really like the idea of my parents staying in my house, criticizing everything, but they are family and I love them.

Mom cocks an eyebrow at me, no doubt hearing what I'm thinking. "We're renting a home here." She casually waves over her shoulder. "I'm thinking about buying the house. It's rather nice and not next door to my sons, who don't like having Mommy and Daddy so close." I roll my eyes.

Ford needs to be here for this conversation. He's going to love having them close. So is Sienna. While she and Mom get along, there's still work to be done between the two of them. I don't think Mom fully respects her yet. Not like Lilah, who seemed to earn her respect a lot faster. I'm sure that has everything to do with Lilah's backbone and personality. Sienna, while an amazing female, isn't one for confrontation unless necessary.

"Would you like to come over for dinner tonight?" Lilah asks. I whip my head in her direction and glare. Who said I wanted my parents over for dinner? Plus, neither one of us likes to cook. We're masters of ordering takeout or eating at one of the many local restaurants.

"We'd love that. Thank you," Dad replies.

"Does six work?" Lilah asks. Dad nods. "Perfect. We'll

see you then."

With my hand still in Lilah's, she turns and tugs me down the beach, back the way we came.

*"Dinner? Really?"* I send to her.

*"If they're considering living here, we should at least share a meal with them. Find out what they're plans are. They'll appreciate it. You are their son."*

*"Ford's going to jump for joy when he hears about them possibly buying something so close to us."*

*"Fortunately for you both, you have plenty of other homes."* She's right, however, I don't want to have to leave here all the time.

*"But this is more of a base for us. We love it here."*

*"I know you do."* She gently squeezes my hand. *"Once everything is settled, I'd love to add some touches to the house."*

Lilah officially moved in with me over the last week. We left her furniture in her apartment and told the landlord she could keep it. She broke her lease, which was no big deal. The fee she had to pay was small. She would have rather waited until the month was ending, but when I reminded her that my money is hers and we have no chance of running out of it anytime soon, she relented.

My mate now resides in Duck with me and I couldn't be happier.

# CHAPTER TWENTY-TWO

## *Lilah*

**DINNER WITH SOL'S PARENTS** WAS INTERESTING. Ford came and brought Sienna. She was going a little stir-crazy in the pack house, not that I've been there yet, so he thought bringing her back home might help. But then Sol's mom got on her about a bunch of little stuff that irritated me until I had to speak up.

It wasn't the smartest thing I'd ever done, but whatever. I couldn't sit there and listen to it any longer. Sienna is very nice, but she isn't as strong as other females. And I don't mean that in the physical sense. She has Ford's strength and other powers. It's her mind that needs building up. Yes, she can hold her own. However, when Eloise would throw a barb at her, she shrank back into herself. Ford didn't stand for it, which was good. I've heard on more than one occasion from Sol's mom how Sienna needs to toughen up. Maybe that's just who Sienna is. We shouldn't have to change to conform to this Verascue set of rules.

"Oh, kitten, you have so much to learn," Sol says from

my side while we watch the sky change as the sun sets.

"So do you. For one, I'm not some timid female. Another thing, I won't back down from anyone. I'm sick of that. Females have been treated as the weaker sex for far too long. You'd think in the paranormal world it would be different since there are so many equals in terms of species and power, but nope."

"Mother isn't treating her as a weaker sex. She's treating her like a weaker paranormal. It has nothing to do with her being a female. She only wants her to rise up and be strong. You should be able to see that."

"I should, but all I saw was Sienna not happy with the way she was talked to."

Sol sighs. "Sienna has to learn to fight her own battles. If you, me, or Ford are always there jumping in, then Mother will never show her the kind of respect she deserves."

"She deserves respect no matter what. She's a part of the family."

"We've been over this, but here it is again," he begins. "My family name is one that instills fear in others in the paranormal world. It also comes with a whole heap of respect. In order to maintain the legacy my parents created, they want their children to have mates worthy of their stature. Mother loves you. Sure, she pushes you, but only because she knows you can take it. I've seen the way she looks at you. It's done with total respect and as someone worthy of being my mate. Now, for my brother, Mother never liked Sienna. Hated is a stronger word." Sol told me about what happened with Ford and Sienna. I can't blame his family for not liking her, but it's in the past. They're mated now and happy. I've seen firsthand how much Ford loves her. "You saying Mother needs to treat her better won't come easily."

"I get it. I just feel bad for Sienna." Luckily, Ford and Sienna went to the pack house and aren't next door to overhear our conversation. "I'd like to go there sometime," I say quietly. "I'm curious as to what all the fuss is about. It's just a pack of wolves."

"A pack of wolves?" Sol snorts then stands. He holds out his hand for me. "Come on. Let's show you what the pack house is like."

"Seriously? Right now?"

He shrugs. "No time like the present."

I stand and take his hand. He's told me a lot about the Avynwood Pack and I've met some of the pack members. But the way he talks about the place makes it sound like a frat house but with families instead of just males.

Sol smiles, then snaps his fingers. We end up in a big open entryway. My eyes widen. The house is stunning, lit with bright lights, and quiet. I don't think I've ever been to a place so nice.

That quiet is broken when a wolf runs into the room.

"So help me, Sevan, I'm going to have your hide for this!" a male yells.

The white wolf with a black snout, tail, and patch on his chest stops in front of us and smiles. I swear to fate his lips lift in a grin. Then a gorgeous female with blonde hair cropped in a pixie cut comes in laughing.

"You better run before Dante catches you," she says.

The wolf nuzzles her hand for a moment until a male with straight black hair that falls past his shoulders comes stomping down the steps with a torn piece of paper in his hand. His face is murderous and his emerald eyes are only on the wolf in front of us. He's close to shifting.

The front door bursts open as another male, this one with hair almost as dark but a leaner frame, comes in and says, "Go. Get out of here."

The wolf—Sevan, I think—wastes no time bolting through the door and away from the house.

The male on the stairs comes down and doesn't stop until he's standing in front of the female. "Your mate is going to be the death of me," he growls.

She smiles up at him, shorter by a solid eight inches at least. "If you didn't start this, he wouldn't have done what he did."

The male growls again then swings his gaze to the one by the door. "And you! You know better, Orion. Why did you have to get involved? He deserved me chewing him out."

Orion smiles. "Like Dalia said, you started it," he says in an exotic accent. Now I remember him. I met so many at the party, but his voice I couldn't forget.

"You've all gone mad!" the male yells.

"Dante, what happened?" Sol asks.

Dante turns to him. "Are you here to mediate? Because if you are, I'm giving up now. You're as bad as the rest of this dysfunctional pack."

Sol pretends to bristle. "I resent that. I'm an excellent judge."

"Fine. Here." He thrusts the paper into Sol's hand.

"What's this?"

"The title to Kaine's car."

"Your one-year-old has a car?"

"It's not any car, you idiot. It's a fully restored 1965 Shelby Cobra."

"So, see if you can get a new title issued." He hands the paper back.

"That's not the point!" Dante yells. "This car was passed down from my father. A male who died thirty years ago. He knew one day I'd have a child and wanted that child to have this car."

"I get it now. The title is sentimental as is the car. But you must have done something to cause Sevan to put his wolf teeth on it."

Dante growls and turns to Dalia. "This is all your fault."

"I don't think so." She's truly gorgeous with her flawless skin and sparkling blue eyes.

Orion comes closer to talk to Sol. "We were having a party and Dante asked Dalia to dance. He leaned in to whisper something to her and Sevan saw red."

"Hold on," Sol says. "You're all mated. Who cares if Dante talked to Dalia?"

"Sevan did," Dalia interjects. "I'm pregnant and he's been wild with jealousy ever since he found out."

"Oooh, that makes sense." Then Sol beams and steps forward to hug her. "Congratulations. I'm so happy for you both."

"Does no one care about my title?" Dante asks, still full of fury.

A female with rich, dark brown hair comes in from a side hallway. Her feet are bare and her jean shorts are frayed at the bottom. She's wearing a white tank top that says, "Females rule. Alphas drool." I've never met her, but I think I love her.

"That shirt is fantastic," I say without thinking. Everyone's eyes swing to me. I offer a little wave.

Sol puts his arm around my waist and draws me close. "For those of you who haven't met her, this is my mate, Lilah. Lilah, this is just a small fraction of the Avynwood Pack. Dante, Dalia, that's Cassie who is the alpha, Aries', mate, and you already met Orion."

"It's nice to meet all of you."

"Lilah wanted to know what the big deal was with the pack, and why Ford and Sienna always come here. I figured it would be best to show her what goes on rather than try to explain it. Lucky for her, you put on a show."

"It's very nice to meet you," Cassie says and dips her head in greeting. Sol must have sent her a message to tell her I'm part fae.

"Can we focus?" Dante asks.

"I'll talk to Cash and Carter and ask them to get you a new title," Cassie states. "But you had to know that getting that close to a pregnant mate was going to cause some kind of issue. Did you forget what it was like when Mira was expecting?" Dante growls. "Exactly. You had tunnel vision. You're the pack beta. Use common sense." She pats him on the cheek. If she were anyone other than the alpha's mate, I don't think she'd get away with that.

"You're lucky I love you," he grumbles, then turns on his heels and stomps back the way he came from.

"This is fun," I say. "I'd love to come here again."

"We just got here, kitten. There's so much to explore."

Cassie laughs. "If you hang out long enough, you'll get the full scope of what happens here. We're a big family and love each other fiercely, but living under the same roof tends to make some of them crazy."

"I can see that. I'm still adjusting to living with Sol and he's only one paranormal."

"He's more like fifty wrapped into one," Orion says with a laugh.

"I thought we were friends," Sol huffs.

Another male suddenly appears in the room. Wake is shirtless with a muscular chest and stomach. Basketball shorts ride low on his hips. His dark brown hair is mussed, and his eyes are focused on Cassie. "Where did you go? The girls are making me insane. They're both hungry, Paige is sleeping, and I don't want to disturb her. Dad has them at the moment, but he's also juggling Quinn."

She steps over and puts a hand on his shoulder. I can clearly see the resemblance in them. "I only came to see if I could find Lealla. She read a new book that she was raving about and never gave me the title."

"You know texting is a thing, right? You didn't have to leave."

"And neither did you. Those are your children, not mine. I have my own to deal with."

"Please," he begs.

Cassie turns to me. "Mom life." She smiles. Wake takes her hand and teleports them both away.

"I gave him that ability, among others." Sol smiles.

"How many times have you sucked on your best friend's neck?" I ask.

He shrugs. "Only when necessary."

I lean in but whisper loudly so there's no doubt everyone hears me. "That's hot."

Sol pulls back with wide eyes to stare at me. "I can't tell if you're playing with me or not."

"I'll tell you later." I wink. In truth, I've always thought two men, two women, threesomes, even more, were sexy. Love is a beautiful thing, regardless of the genders or races of those involved.

Sol leans down and presses his lips to mine in a quick kiss. *"Don't get any ideas. I'm the only one who will share a bed with you."*

I laugh out loud and kiss him back. A throat clearing breaks us apart.

Turning, I find Ford smirking. "Couldn't stay away from me, could you, brother?"

Sol rolls his eyes. "That's right. I just have to be where you are."

"I'm fantastic. It would make sense that you'd always want to be in my company."

"I think you're mistaking that for me. I'm the one who's awesome."

"If your heads get any bigger, you both won't fit in the house," a female voice says. I instantly recognize the paranormal when I see her. Ariane Raines is a force to be reckoned with. She's a strong paranormal and very confident. She's also one of Ford's best friends, so I've seen her a bit while we've been staying in Duck. She usually pops over to visit us after Ford.

Orion walks over to her and pulls her in for a tight embrace and a long kiss on the lips.

"Get a room," Sol groans. "We didn't come here for this."

Ari leans back but doesn't take her hands off her mate as she studies Sol. "No, you came here to show Lilah the pack, and we're part of it, so here we are."

"Get out of my head, female."

"Put a stronger block up and I will." Sol narrows his eyes. "Good job."

We talk a little longer before Ari drags us to the dining

room, where she brings out ice cream and all the toppings to make sundaes. More of the pack join us and I'm introduced around. I never thought I'd want a big family. I have Ness and Don but this… There's something very special about sitting around a table with so many paranormals. The love and care they have for each other is prominent. And there's a strong sense of family that I realize, with an ache in my chest, is something that's been missing in my life.

Sol leans over and takes my hand in his under the table. *"I'm your family now. All these paranormals are as well. We're a big group, misfits and all. And we'll defend one another until the end."*

# CHAPTER TWENTY-THREE

*Solomon*

**FORD AND SIENNA LEAVE** AS WE'RE SAYING goodbye to Orion and Ari. Ari's phone dings with an incoming text in her pocket. She pulls it out and frowns.

"What's going on?" I ask.

"There was an explosion at the Quivakond Pack House. I'm sorry, but we have to go." She reaches for Rion's hand so they can teleport together. Something in my gut tells me we have to go with them.

"We're going, too." Ari nods then leaves. I take Lilah's hand in mine. "I'm not sure what's going on, but please stay near me. I can't have anything happening to you."

She leans over to kiss my cheek. "I will."

I've never taken her to visit the pack where Ari's aunt and uncle live. Sure, I'm very familiar with it. I used to go there frequently. At least they were never bored when I was around.

With a snap of my fingers, I teleport us to the woods surrounding the pack house. I'm not sure where the explosion was, and the last thing I want to do is end up in a pile of burning rubble or on top of someone who's injured.

Hand in hand, we emerge from the woods. It's dark out and cloudy. Luckily, my night vision is fantastic, and I can see things clearly.

Where there was once a front door of the pack house, there's now a hole. The natural, wooden shingles surrounding the area are charred and have water dripping from them. A few hoses lie on the ground, no doubt they were used to extinguish the fire. It's not like they can call the local fire department to put it out. Not only is the home well inside Jacobsburg State Park, but it's also completely hidden by a strong ward. Sure, the pack has cars in a garage nearby, but exposing that and the home would open the pack up so the humans nearby would become aware of their presence.

The Quivakond Pack is one that likes to keep to themselves. Merrick, the pack's alpha, has kept them separate for their safety. They leave to get groceries and other things but mostly stay within the ward. And they're happy that way.

Even with the pack located in eastern Pennsylvania, the ward keeps their weather the same. The seasons can change outside, but within the ward, it's always warm. It was one thing I loved about coming here. It could be the dead of winter and there was warmth and beauty within.

I find Ari standing next to her aunt, Zayda, with a comforting arm around her waist. Zayda has tears running silently down her face. Her long, blonde hair is tucked behind her ears. She's in nothing but a pair of pajama shorts and a T-shirt.

A few feet away, I spot Rion with Merrick. While Zayda looks devastated, Merrick appears murderous. His eyes keep changing colors, alerting those around how his wolf is fighting to break free. Merrick's dark brown hair brushes his shoulders as he turns his head to talk to various members of his pack. He's still in jeans and a T-shirt. His gruff voice can easily be heard over the others. His commanding presence as an alpha is never in question. Nor is his unfailing dedication to his pack. As much as I drove him and his pack crazy, Merrick is a good wolf.

His eyes find mine and he nods. "Solomon, I could use your help."

I nod back and walk toward him with Lilah by my side. "I'm here. Whatever I can do, I will." We might have been at odds before, but I will do anything needed to help.

"One of my females inside is hurt. We've tried to move her, saying we'll bring her to Desmond, but she won't go. She keeps asking for you."

"Me? Why would she ask for me?" Merrick quirks his eyebrow. One name bounces around his mind. It's easy to hear. I don't have to go digging for it.

Tawny is a female I met on one of my trips here. She was different than the others in the pack. Where a lot of the females saw me as a good time and nothing more, Tawny wanted to get to know me. We talked a few times. Okay, so we hooked up twice. Never in the pack house, though. I took her to my place, showed her the amazing skills of Solomon Verascue, and brought her home.

We've kept in touch over the years but nothing crazy. Just two people who shared a mutual attraction and liked to talk. It wasn't just about fooling around. Shock, I know.

She's a younger wolf. Only two hundred and fifty. No mate of her own that I'm aware of. I certainly wasn't him. But I haven't heard from her in about a year or so. I figured she finally found the one for her and that was that. I certainly didn't spend hours pining over her when we weren't together. Not that she wasn't a great shifter, she just wasn't for me. Besides, I wasn't looking for a relationship with someone who wasn't my fated mate.

Merrick's voice breaks through my thoughts. "She's in the dining room. She was in there with some of the other females when the explosion went off. The table landed hard on her. Broke her leg. She refuses to shift. Not even my tone will command her to do so. Maybe you'll have better luck." I nod and start walking toward the house.

"If this were any other time, I'd remind you how I'm your mate, even as another female is calling out for you," Lilah growls in my ear.

I turn and hold her gaze as we keep walking. "You're the only one for me, kitten."

"I know that, but my jealous cheetah isn't having any part of another female wanting you."

I squeeze her hand gently and tug her to a stop. We don't have time for this. I need to get Tawny to shift. But if we go in there and Lilah can't keep her cheetah in check, it will cause more problems. "Let her out quick."

"I don't think that's a great idea."

"It's either that or we'll have a cheetah loose in the pack house. I'd prefer it's done out here and controlled, rather than in there where a lot is going on."

Lilah sighs and acquiesces. In a flash, she's her sleek cheetah. I crouch down and get eye level with her cat.

"I love you both. Not the wolf in there," I tell her. "I don't want anyone else. Please, for me, stay inside Lilah so I can handle this. The quicker we get the wolf to shift, the quicker we find out what happened and if there's any connection to the explosions we've been dealing with." It's a possibility, though I'm not sure how strong of one. The Quivakond Pack has nothing to do with Lilah or me. To have someone here blowing things up doesn't make sense.

Her cheetah steps close and rubs her face against my chin. Reaching up, I stroke the fur on her neck as she brushes against me some more.

"Can you shift back now? We have work to do and I need Lilah."

The cheetah opens her mouth and licks the tip of my nose, causing me to smile. Then she steps back to shift.

With Lilah back in her human form, I stand, take her hand again, and kiss her briefly. She wants to lay her claim on me in front of the pack. These paranormals are new to her. Too bad now isn't the time.

Before we step over the now destroyed threshold of the house, I notice wolves patrolling in my periphery. No doubt they're hunting for foreign scents of whoever did this and making sure no one else gets close.

As we step over the rubble, I hear a female's voice. It's insistent and full of despair. "Tawny, please. You have to shift or let Ari take you to the Avynwood Pack's doctor. I don't want to lose you. You're an important member of this pack."

"Can't. Solomon," Tawny breathes out. She's barely able to say the words. There's no doubt in my mind her lungs are compromised.

We round the corner and I take in the carnage. Where there was once a dining room is splintered wood, glass, and shredded sheetrock. Tawny is on her back with half of the dining room table pushed to the side. Matted brown hair sticks to her forehead as blood trickles down the side of her face. Her left leg is bent up while the other is lying flat to the ground. A quick glance tells me the bones are most likely shattered in the lower right leg.

She hears us as we step over the debris and her eyes latch onto mine. "Sol, you came," she chokes out.

I release Lilah's hand to crouch by Tawny's side. "I did. Now I need you to shift."

Lilah moves to stand directly behind me. Tawny's eyes move up to her and her wolf rises to the surface, eyes flashing emerald green. Well, it won't take much for me to get her to shift. Her wolf surely isn't dormant. "You," she growls with her eyes on my female. "You're not welcome here."

"Anywhere I go, my mate goes," I tell her sternly. No way is she going near Lilah. "She's welcome here by me and your alpha. Now, let's get you to shift."

Her eyes snap back to mine and in them is a fire. I've never seen Tawny jealous before. I'm not quite sure what's going on. We've only been friends. She knew I was with others. We never committed to one another. We were never exclusive.

She reaches up, holding out her hand. It's then I see two red dots on the inside of her wrist.

"You're mated to a vampire?" I ask in astonishment. I'm stunned. She never mentioned it.

"A year ago," she says with struggled breaths in between. Well, that explains why I haven't heard from her. But it doesn't tell me where her mate is and why he isn't here.

She coughs, pulling my focus back. "I need you to shift," I tell her. "I'd rather you do it on your own, but I will force it if I have to. And then you're going to do it a few more times."

She nods ever so slightly and closes her eyes. The shift washes over her, and where her battered body was only a second ago is now a light grey wolf who whimpers as she struggles to stand.

Placing my hand on her fur, I say, "Easy. Shift again. You're still healing." The wolf's emerald eyes hold mine as the shift happens.

I stay by her side as she shifts a handful of times before she's back, fully healed, in her human form. As soon as she is, she throws herself into my arms. I'm caught off guard and tumble back to the ground, landing hard on a piece of wood. Thank fate for my super vampire healing. I don't look good in shades of blue and purple. Bruises don't complement my complexion.

It takes Lilah all of two seconds before she's there, peeling the shifter off me, only Tawny doesn't go far. Seems her vampire mate gave her his strength. No matter. Lilah has the Verascue power in her on top of her fae and cheetah lineage. There's no other shifter who could best my mate, even one with vampire strength.

I stand, since I don't have a female on me, and move to Lilah's side. Her eyes are sapphire blue as they stay trained on the female before her. My hand rests on the small of Lilah's back as I lean in close so I can speak right in her ear. If I don't get her to calm down, there's going to be some major bloodshed. "Kitten, you need to relax. I've told you. I'm yours. Rein it in, baby."

Lilah leans toward me and puts a possessive hand in mine, though her eyes never leave Tawny's. "I suggest you keep your hands off my mate," Lilah growls. "Lest you forget how possessive shifters can be. I will rip your limbs from your body without ever having to touch you."

Tawny laughs. "Sol's good, but he doesn't have that kind of power to give you."

"No, he doesn't, but my mother did. I'm not only a cheetah and have every single one of Sol's powers, but I'm also fae. I can cut you down before you can blink. So if I were you, I'd back it up before we have to send your body to your mate in a bag and explain how you stepped over a line you knew better than to cross."

# CHAPTER TWENTY-FOUR

## *Lilah*

**THERE ARE DAYS WHEN** I LOOK AT OTHER paranormals and honestly can't believe how stupid they are. Like this shifter in front of me. Is she serious right now? I could kill her with a flick of my wrist. Not that I've done that before, but she doesn't need to know that. There are fae out there who have.

She also doesn't need to know how young and inexperienced I am. I have enough false bravado to pull it off. Plus, there's the fact that my cheetah wants to rip her to shreds for clinging to my mate as she did. It's like she doesn't have a clue what it's like to be mated. How can she be all over what's mine when she has a mate of her own? And where is her mate, for that matter? You'd think her male would be with her.

"I'm not afraid of you," she growls.

"Here we go," Sol mutters under his breath. He has to feel the anger rolling off me. Not only that, he can easily read my mind.

"One hand, that's all it will take," I say through clenched teeth. "You lay one hand on him, and I'll kill you where you stand."

The female standing behind Tawny looks like she isn't sure whether to shift and protect her packmate or move back because she has it coming.

The male I saw outside earlier comes in. His boots stomp over the floor, not caring what he's crushing on his way. His dark brown hair flows around him like a small curtain as he moves. Power, grace, it's all there plus the obvious commanding presence of an alpha. "Tawny, enough," he growls as his eyes flash emerald. "You will not fight Solomon's mate. He came here and saved you by helping you shift, and you repay him by disrespecting the mate bond? Shame on you. Now, back down."

Tawny's eyes flick from Sol to the alpha and back again before she hesitantly takes two steps back and drops her head in submission. At least she isn't stupid enough to go against him. Though, I think the jury is still out on her level of idiocy.

The male turns toward us. "My apologies for my pack member." Sol nods but I don't move. My hands are still splayed, ready to hit Tawny with as much magic as I can muster. The alpha sets his gaze on me. "I didn't get a chance to properly introduce myself. I'm Merrick, the alpha of the Quivakond Pack."

"Lilah Verascue. Nice to meet you." I nod in greeting and Merrick doesn't bother offering his hand. At least he took my cue and decided not to try to touch me.

Sol nudges my side and says with his mind, *"You using my last name is so freaking hot. Can you do that again later when we're in bed?"*

I turn to glare at him. *"Seriously? We're standing in a pack house that had a bomb go off in it, and all you can think about is sex?"*

He shrugs. *"What can I say? I'm an excellent multitasker."*

*"I don't even know how to respond to that."*

Ari comes into the room with the woman I saw her with outside. Reading Sol's mind for the first time since we got here, I find out that it's Ari's aunt and the alpha's mate, Zayda.

"Do you have any idea who did this?" Ari asks.

"None," Merrick replies. "No one in the pack picked up any scents and no one inside saw or heard anything. A lot of the pack were upstairs in their bedrooms. Others were in the dining room or kitchen."

The female behind Tawny speaks up. "We were just sitting here and then all of a sudden there was an explosion." She trembles as tears form in her eyes. "Tawny… I thought she was going to die."

Tawny finally shakes herself out of her Solomon induced stupor and goes to her friend's side to wrap an arm around her. "I'm okay."

"Yes, now. Thanks to the vampire."

"I have a name," Sol interjects. "A fabulous name that the world should recognize."

"Your ego knows no bounds," Merrick says dryly.

"It's one of my many gifts."

"Can we focus?" Ari asks. "There's a freaking hole in the front of the house and you morons are talking about Sol's ego."

"Hey!" Sol calls out. "Be careful with my ego. It could use a little stroking now and then." He turns to me and pins me with a pointed glare. For fate's sake.

Ari stomps forward and gets in Sol's face. "So help me, Solomon Verascue, I will teleport your vampire butt home and slap handcuffs on you." She's talking about the magical handcuffs paranormals can't break out of. At least I think she is, but Sol has other ideas.

"That sounds pretty kinky. Do you think Rion would be on board with that? I've been known to have multiple partners in the past, but never anyone who's mated. Unless you two swing that way. Male, female, I'm game." He waggles his eyebrows. Thank fate I can read his mind and pick out which parts he's serious about and which he isn't. He does think it sounds kinky and gender doesn't matter to him. The memories I've gotten of his… Multiple partners are right. But he has no interest in Ariane or Orion.

I reach over and slap my hand over his mouth. Instead of trying to struggle free, he licks my palm, eliciting a chill which races up my spine in the most delicious way.

*"You're going to be the death of me,"* I tell him with my mind.

*"Nah, but I am going to make you see stars later."*

Ari throws her hands up in the air. "I give up! Go home, Sol. You're nothing but a distraction."

He pulls my hand away. "I'm not going anywhere. Someone blew up this house. It's all too familiar with what's been going on with us."

"Then for the love of all that is good, focus! Stop steering the conversation down the wrong path."

"You're no fun," he pouts.

Ari ignores him and turns to Merrick. She then gives him a quick rundown of what's been happening to Sol and me, and how we have no idea who's doing it.

Merrick strokes his full beard, which matches his hair. "The paranormal responsible, and I'm assuming it's a paranormal since they've followed you, why would they come here? I have no ties to either of you outside of the utter annoyance I have every time Sol has visited."

"I'd say I resent that, but that would be a lie," Sol states.

"If it's the same paranormal, coming here would mean they aren't after me," I say, rolling everything over in my mind, trying to find a common factor. Merrick has a point about it being a paranormal.

Ari claps her hands together, drawing our attention to her. "What if they're after the paranormals Sol has been with? They went after Lilah. Tawny is obviously one of Sol's conquests."

"Hey!" Tawny interjects, offended.

"Oh, whatever," Ari replies, waving her off. "Maybe they're trying to pick off those he's been intimate with."

"They better be immortal because that list is long," Sol says, drawing out the last word.

I turn toward him and put my hand on my hip. "Could we not talk about the thousands of paranormals you've taken to bed?"

"They weren't always in a bed, kitten. Sometimes they were up against a wall or bent over a couch. Oh! There was this one time, I was with this female on a Ferris wheel. It was dark out and when we got to the top I—"

"Sol!" I yell.

"Sorry, kitten." He has enough sense to realize what he was saying and looks sheepish. "You're the only one for me."

"Save it," I growl. I have zero desire to hear about the different ways he's screwed other females.

*"Not always females. Mostly, but not always,"* he says in my mind.

My only reaction is to stomp my foot. I couldn't care less who he was with. I still don't want to hear about it. My cheetah certainly doesn't want to. Freaking jealousy.

"Just when I think you can't get stupider, you do," Ari observes.

"Say that's true," Merrick interjects, getting us back on topic. "Say they're after others you've been with, there's no way to warn them all."

"Or find them all," Sol adds. "You think I remember every single one of them?" He scoffs. "I have a good memory, but it's not that good."

I zone out for a bit and rattle my mind, trying to find something. I feel like there's a piece I'm missing—the final piece of the puzzle. It's right there just out of reach.

The conversation around me continues, but I step away to look at the rubble. I walk along the border of the destruction, outside and back in again, determined to figure it out.

In the dining room, I notice Tawny and the other female are missing. "Where did they go?" I ask.

"To bed," Zayda says. "Tawny needs rest." I nod.

There's something about Tawny I don't like, and it's not just the fact that she obviously has the hots for my mate.

Quietly, I slip away again, but this time I walk up the stairs of the pack house. I let the sound of multiple voices wash over me until I latch on to the one I'm searching for.

Four doors down on the right, I find Tawny's room. She's talking to the other female. Luckily, no one else is around and I can eavesdrop.

"Where's Trent?" the other female asks. "He should be here looking out for you. I can't believe he hasn't shown up yet. He must have felt your pain."

"We don't have a typical relationship. Not everything is the same as it is when two shifters mate." She's right. When different species mix, there's no certainty as to what will happen with the mate bond and what won't. Some things could click into place, others not.

"Still, you should contact him. He should be made

aware that you almost died."

"I will. I just need sleep first."

I take a moment to go prying into their minds. First, I dive into the female with her. Nothing much there except fear and concern for her friend. Then I dive into Tawny's. The sheer level of her need for Sol has my fingers splaying and my cheetah rising to the surface. This female needs to realize he doesn't want her like that. Why can't she take a hint? He's mated now. He'll never want anyone other than me for the rest of his life. She has to understand how that works. She's mated after all.

Rooting around a bit more, I look for memories of her mate. There. I found some. He's tall with silver hair cut short. Chiseled jaw. Strong cheekbones. Striking, if I'm honest with myself. He's not hard on the eyes. He's muscular but lean, and he looks at her like she's his next meal.

I sift around a bit, trying to avoid the memories of what it felt like when he drank from her. I don't need to see that. No one does. But then I come across something else. It's her hovering over his body. His neck is bent at an angle that isn't natural, and there's a silver stake in his chest. I gasp loudly without thinking of the ramifications.

The conversation in the bedroom stops. They must have heard me. Quickly, I dart down the hall and descend the stairs. My footfalls are nearly soundless as I move. The door to the bedroom opens as I'm halfway down the stairs, but I don't stop moving until I'm standing beside Sol.

He turns and eyes me curiously. He must search my mind and find what I saw upstairs inside of Tawny's head, because a muscle in his jaw ticks.

He turns back to Merrick. "If you don't mind, I'm going to take my mate home. This has been a lot for her."

"Of course," Merrick replies.

Sol laces our fingers and snaps to get us out of there before Ari has a chance to read our minds. I'm aware of how powerful she is. While she can't knock down the wall in Sol's head, she might be able to in mine. I have his powers, though I haven't mastered them yet.

We land in the living room in our house in Duck. Sol grips my upper arms and looks into my mind as he thoroughly goes through everything I heard and saw. With every passing second, his jaw tenses more to the point I think he might crack his teeth.

"Do you know him?" I ask. "The vampire she's mated to?"

Sol nods. "He's my cousin."

# CHAPTER TWENTY-FIVE

*Solomon*

**"YOUR WHAT?" LILAH YELLS.**

A second later, Ford and Sienna appear. "I heard yelling. What happened?" Ford asks, eyes darting around, shoulders tense.

I take a few minutes to relay everything that happened tonight, including the revelation that Tawny is mated to our cousin, Trent.

"Hold on," Ford says and turns to Lilah. "You saw him dead in her mind? Are you sure it wasn't a dream she had and not a memory? Sometimes those two can get confusing when you're reading someone's mind."

"I'm honestly not sure what it was," she replies. "As soon as I saw it, I hightailed it out of there, or they would have caught me."

"And no one thought to ask Tawny for the truth? Sol, you could have easily read her mind and found out if it happened or not."

"I'm sorry, brother. I was a little shocked to see our cousin on a bed with a broken neck and a stake in his chest. Shook me a little. I did the first thing I could think of, which was get my mate away from the female who may or may not have murdered our cousin," I seethe. It's like Ford doesn't even know me, or what it's like to be mated. We take care of our females first then deal with any situation after. They are always our top priority.

"I'm sorry," he says, and rakes his fingers through his hair. "Of course, you wanted to get Lilah out of there, but we need to go back to question her."

"I'm going to visit Mother and see if she has any idea where Trent is. I want to make sure he's safe before I confront Tawny. As far as she's aware, we don't know what's in her head."

"How can you be certain you'll even be able to find her? She could run."

I cock an eyebrow and Lilah let's out a long sigh. "She threw herself at Sol," Lilah says. "Not like a 'Hey, thanks for saving my life,' type of thing but a 'Thank fate, you're here. I love you so much!' thing."

"Well, brother," Ford starts. "You sure do leave the females wanting more."

Sienna slaps him on the stomach with the back of her hand. "Really?"

"Sorry, honey. I was just stating the obvious. You've seen the way females hang on him. Do you remember when we were in the Bahamas and found that little bar right on the beach? Sol made it his mission to get the bartender back to his place. Then for the rest of the trip she followed him around like a puppy." He chuckles as he remembers. I can't help but smile. That female was good in bed. However, I don't like clingy. Can't handle it. Except for Lilah. She could drape herself over me for all I care. Actually, I'd like that very much.

"You're as bad as your brother!" Lilah yells at Ford.

"The two of you drift off topic faster than anyone I've ever seen."

I walk over to the fridge, realizing how hungry I am. I can't remember the last time I ate. "Get used to it, kitten. You have the rest of your life to deal with me."

Opening the door, I reach in and pull out a jar of olives and a package of hard salami I got at the grocery store a few days ago. I close the door and place both items on the counter then open the lid to the olives. Not bothering with a fork or spoon to get them out, I reach in and use my fingers to pluck one free and pop it into my mouth. When I look up, everyone is watching me.

"What?" I ask mid-chew.

"Did you forget about Trent?" Lilah asks.

"No," I lie. I totally forgot. We were talking about the Bahamas, then my stomach growled. I couldn't ignore that. I doubt Lilah wants me feasting on her at the moment.

Ford looks over and sees what I have. He comes to stand by my side and opens the package of sliced salami. "Did you at least spring for the good stuff this time and not the store brand?"

"Hey, there's nothing wrong with the store brand."

"You have more money than you could ever spend, yet you cut costs on lunch meat."

I pick up a piece of salami and grab another olive. I roll the olive up in it. Ford scrunches his nose at it as I shove the food into my mouth in one bite. "So good," I say while chewing.

"Are you two serious right now?" Lilah asks.

"This is commonplace," Sienna interjects. "They're like squirrels. It takes a lot for them to stay focused on one thing. Sol was distracted by his stomach and Ford was distracted by the sight of food. If we wave something equally enticing at them, they'll come back this way."

"So, I should lift my shirt and flash them?"

Sienna chuckles. "I think that will only work on Sol, but it might be enough to break Ford's food trance as well."

"You know we can hear you, right?" Ford asks.

"Oh, we know." Sienna smiles.

Lilah strides over and takes the olive jar, puts the lid on it, grabs the salami as I'm taking another piece out of it, and seals the bag. She opens the refrigerator and puts both inside then turns to us. "You can both eat after we find out if your cousin is alive or not. You're immortal. You won't die if you don't get your lunch meat fix for an hour."

"Speak for yourself," I reply. "I'm about to wither away over here." I lift my shirt and flash her my clearly defined abs. "See! I'm deteriorating before our very eyes!"

She drops her gaze to my stomach and licks her lips. I know what I have and how much females love the muscles I hide under my clothes. Sometimes clothing is optional. I've been known to stroll around naked. If you have it, flaunt it.

Ford claps his hands, drawing Lilah out of her trance a moment before her hand touches my stomach. She shakes her head. "Right. We need to go."

I smirk. "I'm not the only one who gets easily distracted."

"Yeah, well, you were distracted by food and I was distracted by your body. They're very different."

"I don't think so, kitten. They're both delicious."

She rolls her eyes and looks toward the sky. "Why, fate? Why did you pair me with this male out of every other paranormal in the world?"

Sienna laughs. "Admit it. You don't for one second regret being mated to him."

Lilah drops her head and her eyes meet mine. "I don't," she says honestly.

"All right then," Ford states. "If we don't go now, my brother will be sucking on your neck and we'll never get anywhere."

I clear my throat, trying to tamp down the jolt of lust that traveled south along with the blood in my upper body. "Let's go to Amalfi and see if we can find our parents. We need to locate Trent."

I take Lilah's hand in mine as Ford walks over to Sienna. "Pool?" I ask.

"Pool." Ford nods.

We both snap our fingers and appear a second later, standing on the stone patio of my parents' villa in Amalfi. There's no one outside and the sky is overcast with dark clouds approaching. A storm is rolling in and thunder can be heard in the distance.

We move forward to the stairs that lead up from the patio to the house. Lilah doesn't release my hand as we go.

"This place is stunning," she says in awe.

"It is. It's my parents' main home." A thought hits me. They may still be in the Outer Banks. They said they were thinking about buying a home there.

Ford stops mid-step and spins a few stairs above me where he stands. "Don't you think you should have told me that?" he yells.

"Oh, I'm sorry. I was a little caught up in trying to stay alive instead of relaying the information about our parents to you."

The door to the home opens and my mom comes out. She's dressed in a flowing magenta dress with spaghetti straps and heart-shaped neckline. Yes, I'm familiar with some fashion terminology. When you've been around long enough, you absorb nuggets of information.

"Next time I think of purchasing a home, I'll send up a flare," she states very matter-of-fact. "Or maybe a carrier pigeon. Would that do?"

Ford turns to her. "A simple call would suffice."

"I wasn't aware I needed to run everything by you. I'll make a note of it for any future transactions." She rolls her eyes. Well, if there's one thing the Verascue women have in common, it's the ability to master the eye roll.

We continue up the steps and follow her inside where we find Dad on the couch with a newspaper in hand. Putting it down, he smiles as we come into the room. "What a nice surprise. To what do we owe the pleasure?" At least they weren't doing something I'd rather never see.

Ford cuts right to the chase. "When was the last time you saw Trent?"

My mom cocks her head to the side to study him then moves her gaze to me then Lilah. She's reading her mind. I watch as realization dawns on her. Her mouth sets in a firm line.

Trent is one of only two cousins I have. My aunt was my mother's sister. She and my uncle died about seven hundred years ago. It was awful. I'd never seen my mom so upset. Ford never got to meet them. He would have loved them, too. They were both so warm and friendly. Trent and his sister, Genevieve, are the only ones left on that side of the family, besides my mother. My dad has an estranged brother he hasn't heard from in a thousand years.

"Seth, we need to go. I have to check on him," Mom says with a slight tremble in her voice. It's not easy to rattle her, but this has her truly shaken.

Dad comes over and grips her hand in his then faces us. "Trent lives in Ottawa currently. Last we heard he was doing fine there, but it's been a while."

"No mention of Tawny and her being his mate?" I ask. Dad shakes his head.

Quickly, he sends Ford and me the location. Specifically, the interior of Trent's home so we can teleport right into it.

"I'm not sure what we're going to be stepping into," Dad says. "Be careful. Guards up."

Ford turns to Sienna. "Will you stay here? I don't want to put you in harm's way."

Sienna lifts her hand to cup Ford's cheek. "I'm safest with you. Besides, I have almost every one of your powers now. I can take care of myself."

Ford removes her hand from his cheek and kisses her palm. "I can't lose you again."

"You won't." The moment is so sweet and so real. Ever since the two of them reunited, they don't hold their emotions back, regardless of where they are or who's in their presence. My brother is more peaceful than he's ever been in his life and it's all thanks to the female in front of him.

He laces their fingers and nods to the rest of us. "On three."

Together, we count down and snap at the same time. If we're going to drop in on something or come under attack, we're going to do it together.

We land in a darkened, very quiet home. The drapes in the living room are pulled shut, but I can still make out every detail in the room. Carefully, we step forward and go toward different parts of the house. Mom and Dad head toward the bedrooms, Ford and Sienna toward the basement, and Lilah and I toward the kitchen.

We're two steps in when a loud wail pierces the air. I

don't think before I'm running in the direction of the sound, with Lilah in tow. We stop as soon as we cross the threshold to the master bedroom. There, on the bed, is Trent. The stake has been removed but the blood from where it was is present. His neck is broken, his head lying crooked.

Mom drops to her knees on the carpet as Dad follows suit to sweep her into his arms as sobs wrack her body. She's loved Trent like a son. Ever since the death of her sister and brother-in-law, she was always there for my cousins. And now Trent is gone.

I choke back tears as I look at Trent. I can't believe he's dead. I was hoping it wasn't real. That whatever Lilah saw was just a dream Tawny remembered. To think she could do something like this.

Ford and Sienna come into the room. Sienna lets out a muffled cry as she covers her mouth with her hand.

Then I notice something in Trent's hand. Walking over, I peer down and see something I would recognize anywhere. It's a necklace my mom gave me for one of my birthdays. It's a simple, thin platinum chain. But what makes it unique is the design of the chain. Mom had it made for me in Italy. The links are nothing like I'd ever seen, making it completely original.

I've never given it to anyone. I've never removed it from the box it's been in for the majority of my life. I wore it for a while but was afraid I'd lose it, so I tucked it away, safe in my bedroom. A bedroom a certain female was in after the last time I saw the necklace.

I remember taking it out and admiring it before safely tucking it away again. A few days later, Tawny came over. It was the second time I slept with her. She must have taken it. The question is, why did she give it to Trent?

# CHAPTER TWENTY-SIX

*Lilah*

**SOL STARES AT SOMETHING** IN TRENT'S HAND. A necklace, I think.

"Can one of you go get Kylest?" he asks. "I'll text Raven to find out where they are. There's a way certain fae can communicate with someone deceased. Maybe communicate isn't the right word. Pull their last memories. But the soul has to still be with the body."

I gape. "Are you serious?"

Ford cuts in, "Kylest mentioned it to me once. It's possible. I wonder when this happened."

"We'll see if we can find out," Sol states as his fingers fly over the screen of his phone. He waits for a few beats. "Raven said they're home. Can one of you get him?" he asks his parents.

"I will," Seth says. He kisses Eloise on the forehead before releasing her and stands. A moment later he's gone.

Eloise wipes the tears from her face and slowly stands. Ford reaches out to help her, but she waves him off. Stepping forward, she slowly sits down on the bed next to Trent.

"Sweet male, what happened to you? I'm so sorry I wasn't here to protect you. I promised your parents I would always look out for you and your sister if something happened to them. I didn't do my job. I'll regret it for the rest of my life." Her tone turns vengeful. "And when I find out who did this, I will end their life for what they did to you."

"I have a feeling it was Tawny, but I need to be sure," Sol states. "That's why I'm asking Ky over here. I don't want her to see us coming. And we will go for her if she did this. There won't be a place on this planet or in any realm she'll be able to hide."

Seth reappears with Kylest and Raven. Kylest's hair is pink and Raven's is a solid black.

Kylest releases Raven's hand and steps toward the bed. "May I?" he asks Eloise gently.

She nods and stands to allow Kylest to get closer. He hovers his hand over Trent's face and closes his eyes. Reaching down, he gently places his fingers on Trent's temple and doesn't say a word.

Minutes tick by. Kylest doesn't move. Nothing is said as we watch and wait. I hope we get some answers. Sol and his family shouldn't have to go through this. This poor male on the bed didn't deserve to die. I've seen into Sol's mind since we got here. There are so many memories of Trent. Sol might have a brave face on, but I can feel his sorrow and anguish where it resides in the center of my chest. It's taking everything in me not to reach out and comfort him. He doesn't want that now, though. He wants revenge and I can't blame him. When he does break down, I'll be there for him. I'll always be there for my mate.

Kylest finally withdraws his hand and shakes his head before standing and turning to face us. "A female named

Tawny murdered him. Before it happened, she spoke of how much she loved him and how they were mates. Yet, he didn't feel the connection. Nevertheless, she convinced him over months to gift her some of his powers. Trent wasn't a weak vampire. She was eventually equal to him in some ways, and when she surprised him with a hit to the head, he didn't have time to heal before she staked him in the chest."

"I'm going to murder her," Eloise seethes. She turns to Sol. "She's at the Quivakond Pack House, correct?"

"Yes, but you can't go in there and murder one of the pack," Sol says. "Let me talk to Merrick first." Eloise's eyes are wild. She wants revenge, however, we have to try and keep the peace as much as possible. The pack has been through a lot already. "If you go there and murder her without speaking to Merrick first, you're going to have an entire pack of wolves attacking you. I have no desire for more blood to be shed."

Seth lays a hand on Eloise's shoulder. "He's right. We all want this female dead, but we have to respect the pack as well. Let Sol and Ford go ahead of us. Give them a five-minute head start then we'll go."

Sol nods. "That or I'll kill her first."

Eloise's gaze snaps to Sol's. "You don't touch her. Vengeance will be mine."

"It's because of me she's even familiar with our family," he says, his voice gradually getting louder. "It's my fault, so I should be the one to kill her." All the while my cheetah is inside me prowling, waiting for her own taste of the wolf's blood. This should be interesting. I wonder how many of us can kill her at once.

Seth interjects. "You'll wait five minutes, son. Then, when we're all there, we can take turns ripping her to pieces." His fangs descend and it's the first time I'm seeing just how vicious Sol's father can be. He's very friendly, very calm, but now, I see the other side of him.

"Deal," Sol says and grips my hand in his. He turns to Ford. "Front yard." Ford nods and grips Sienna's hand in his.

The four of us teleport and each land in the front yard of the pack house Sol and I were at earlier. There are a few of the pack putting huge wood panels on the front of the house to cover up the large hole. I don't miss the wolves patrolling nearby.

We step forward, but Merrick and Zayda meet us outside. "Sol, what are you doing back here?" Merrick asks.

Instead of speaking out loud, Sol steps forward and holds Merrick in his gaze. I have no doubt he's relaying everything to him. We wouldn't want Tawny to hear him and run. Of course, she could have run by now. Who knows?

I watch as Merrick's eyes narrow then go emerald green. They don't flash. No, they stay that way, letting all of us see how close his wolf is to the surface. Sol doesn't break eye contact. I'm not sure what else he's saying, but another minute goes by and Merrick's eyes return to their natural color.

They both nod and Sol turns to me to speak in my mind. *"I'm going to go inside and find Tawny. Once I do, you can join us. But I need to know she won't be leaving. Me alone she won't run from. Adding you to the mix might make her a flight risk, especially now that she can teleport. Give me a thirty-second head start. Come up quietly with Merrick and the others."*

*"Okay. But, Sol? Be careful. She might not be as powerful as you and only has love in her eyes where you're concerned, but she's dangerous. We don't know if she has more silver stakes up there with her."*

*"I will, kitten. I promise."*

Sol turns and relays everything to Ford. Then he's off toward the front of the house. We count to thirty in our minds and follow him. I'm first up the steps with Merrick at my back then Ford, Sienna, and Zayda. None of us make noise as we go.

I hear them before I see them. I follow their voices to the room I was outside earlier.

"Sol, it's so nice of you to come back," Tawny says.

"I had to make sure you're okay. I don't want to see anything happen to you." The lie drips off his tongue like honey.

"I'm okay. Honest."

When I round the corner into the room, I notice Sol's arms around her. Her eyes widen as we each file into the room. Sol moves his hands over her fingers, effectively preventing her from teleporting.

Ford and I both hone in on her and stare her down. I have no doubt he's probing her mind as I am. She can't block us. Our powers are stronger.

Memories, actions, ideas flash around. Nothing I saw before. Maybe I would have had I stayed longer. But what I see now causes my breath to falter and my chest to feel tight.

"You were the one who tried to kill me?" I whisper. "You set off all those bombs?"

Tawny sneers. Even with the group of us in the room, she thinks she's won. She doesn't realize Sol is restraining her. She thinks he's holding her hands. If I weren't so full of rage, I'd laugh.

"You don't belong with Solomon," she spits. "He's mine and always has been."

I try to keep myself calm as I voice more of my

findings. "Trent wasn't your mate, was he? That mark on your wrist is nothing more than a magically spelled tattoo. Why go after him? Why pull him into this madness?" There's no point in hiding what happened. We can easily read her mind.

"I needed Sol's strength. With Ford being mated and Sol not giving it to me, the only one left was his cousin. I had to try and convince him he was my mate. His power is mine now."

Sol leans away but doesn't release her. The anguish is clear in his voice when he speaks. "Why did you kill him? He was my blood. My family."

She tries to shake him free, finally realizing she's caught and can't break the hold. "He wasn't you, Sol," she says sweetly. "I only wanted you."

"So you killed him? You blew up the bar, my homes? You blew up your pack's home?"

"I was trying to kill her so I could have you to myself," she juts her chin toward me. "But with the wards up, I got as close as I could. I might not have been able to get into your home in New Jersey, but I could lob a grenade at the door."

Waves of anger start coursing off Sol. His pain has turned to hatred. "How did you know about that house?"

She smiles still trying to be sweet. "Trent. Your family has a lot of secrets but, luckily for me, he was willing to part with them. Well, not really. I read that mind of his as I slept with him one last time."

Sol hisses as his fangs descend. Tawny tips her head to the side, offering her neck. Does she actually think Sol is going to drink from her? He's about to kill her.

A split second later, Eloise and Seth enter the room along with Kylest and Raven. There's no escaping now. Not that there was before they showed up.

Fear doesn't leech into Tawny's eyes until they land on Sol's parents. Then she quickly turns to Merrick. "Please," she begs. "It was self-defense. I swear. Trent was going to hurt me. I did what I had to so I could save myself." Seriously? He's been in the room the whole time. He heard what she said. I guess when faced with Eloise and Seth Verascue, you do what you can to protect yourself.

"Enough," Merrick snaps. "What you did was inexcusable. I will not help you. I will not fight for you. You're lucky I don't kill you myself for what you did. But I promised the Verascue family their vengeance, and that's what they'll have."

Voices in the hallway alert me to the crowd that's gathered, but no one in here cares. Everyone has their eyes on one shifter alone. And she's about to understand what it means to be on the wrong side of the Verascue family

# CHAPTER TWENTY-SEVEN

## *Solomon*

**NOW THAT I'M STANDING** IN FRONT OF TAWNY and reading her mind, so much has been revealed. So much I wish I didn't see. Like her killing Trent. It makes my chest ache as anger courses through me. I can't believe she did that to him.

He must have seen it coming. He had my necklace in his hand, which he got from Tawny. It was a message; of that I have no doubt. Because Trent would have known who that belonged to. He was there when I received it.

I didn't see him take it off her in her memories because she didn't realize he did. They fought the night of his death before he went to sleep. He was jealous over the way she still thought of me. One thing that settles my mind, a fraction, is that Trent knew me and knew I'd never screw around with someone that was his. He threw that back at her at one point. How he knew me better, and no matter how much she wanted me, if I were aware of the fact that they were together, I would never touch her. That seemed to incite her more. Maybe it was the tipping point in her mind.

From what I could tell, she never loved him. Was simply using him to gain power so she could have me. She never thought I'd reject her. The problem Tawny never saw coming was Lilah. Once Lilah became my mate, Tawny did whatever she could to get rid of her.

I still can't believe she tattooed a vampire's mate mark on her arm. The one Lilah and Sienna proudly wear since they're our mates. It was a low blow to make everyone think she was mated. Once she had those, everyone was fooled.

I once asked Sienna what happened to her mate mark with Eli. It was gone from her wrist once she finally accepted Ford back into her life. She said up until then it was there and when she decided to give herself to Ford, it was gone. She missed it obviously, but she was determined to start a new life with my brother. I wasn't aware that mate marks could disappear. It was something new I learned.

My mom's voice breaks my thoughts. "Thank you, Merrick. We'll take her from here." Mom nods to me and lays her hand on my shoulder. She teleports us away.

Glancing around, I realize we landed in the woods behind Ford's house in Portland, Oregon. It's quiet and on fifteen acres. No one will see what we're going to do to Tawny.

Everyone else appears: Dad, Lilah, Ford, Sienna, Kylest, and Raven. Ky uses his magic to put us in a soundproof dome. Now Tawny can scream as loud as she wants and no one will hear her.

I focus back on her. Tawny's eyes are wide and her body trembles where I hold her hands so she can't teleport away. Yes, she's strong. She has Trent's power, but she's no match for me.

"Please, Solomon," she begs. "Don't let them hurt me."

I laugh a humorless laugh. "You think I'm going to save you? You must be desperate. I'm the last paranormal you should turn to."

My mom walks around us until she's standing directly behind Tawny. Her perfectly manicured fingers wrap around Tawny's neck as she hisses in her ear. "You broke my nephew's neck. I'm going to do the same to you. Too bad he didn't give you the power to heal. You'll feel every ounce of pain as we tear you apart, one appendage at a time."

Tawny whimpers in fear as her eyes well with tears.

"You did this to yourself," I remind her. "No one made you kill Trent. No one forced you to make the bombs you used to try to blow my mate to pieces or the grenades you threw. That was all you. And now you'll pay the price."

Mom takes that as her cue to snap her neck. She doesn't try to sever it from her body or do anything else. She wants Tawny to feel the pain.

Tawny blinks as she stands there with a broken neck, unable to heal without shifting. She tries to call upon her wolf, her eyes turning green, but I speak with my mind right to her wolf. I will her into submission and tell her to resist the shift. Tears flow from Tawny's eyes, but she can't speak. Now it's my turn.

I lift her fingers in mine and tear her thumbs from her hands. Blood pours from them as she cries harder. Then I do the same with her other fingers—one at a time. I want her to suffer.

Lilah steps up to my side. I nod to her and she takes position in front of me. My mom still at Tawny's back.

Lilah shifts into her cheetah and forcefully jumps at Tawny. Mom steps away to allow Tawny to fall to the ground with a hard thud. Tawny tries to scream. Tries to move, all to no avail. Lilah's cheetah opens her mouth, letting her ferocious teeth show a second before bending down and puncturing Tawny's femoral artery. Blood pours from her and pools on the ground. Lilah's cheetah moves to the other leg but instead of neatly piercing the skin, she rips a chunk of flesh away.

Her cheetah steps back then shifts into human Lilah.

It's my dad's turn now. He doesn't say a word as he takes his time removing all four of Tawny's limbs from her body. The blood coating the ground expands. She's still alive. Barely.

The death blow comes from my mom. It's only right since she feels responsible for Trent. Even though he was a fully capable vampire, her pain rings loudly in her mind and she doesn't try to shield it.

My mom feels guilty about what happened. Feels that she could have done something to prevent it. But if that guilt is to lay on anyone, it's me. I'm the one who brought Tawny into our family. I thought I could trust her as a friend. It goes to show that I need to keep my guard up. Protect who's mine better. Only trust those close to me, the ones who have my back when I need them to.

Mom steps over her, her legs on either side of Tawny's torso, her heels sinking into the blood surrounding her. Mom bends down to squat over her and looks in Tawny's eyes. "I don't believe in heaven or hell, but I hope to fate wherever you're going, you suffer there. I hope your soul never rests. I hope you have an eternity of pain." Then she hooks her nail in Tawny's shirt, and pulls, opening it up. Mom's hand settles over Tawny's heart as she digs her nails into her flesh.

Mom isn't going to make it quick. She slowly pushes her fingers into Tawny's chest until she grasps the organ somehow still beating behind her ribs. She squeezes. Tawny's eyes go wide as she gasps for breath until more blood pours out from the open wound. Mom crushes her heart, rendering it useless. A moment later, Tawny's body is listless and dead. There's no life left. There's no coming back from everything we've done to her.

Mom stands and moves back. Ky is there, quick to spin his magic, removing the blood from her, a second before she collapses into my dad's arms and cries.

"Kylest, can you torch Tawny up and use your magic to clear the area of any residual blood once she's gone?" Ford asks. Ky nods.

I turn and find Sienna with her face buried in my brother's neck. Sienna might be one of us now, but she doesn't like death or bloodshed. She would much rather have peace in our world. Ford's arms are wrapped around her as he holds her close, shielding her from the carnage.

With a few flicks of Ky's wrist, Tawny's body is engulfed in flames that spread to the blood surrounding her, as if it were gasoline fueling the blaze. I stand watching it with zero remorse. If only I could have put a stop to this before it got Trent killed. If only I had known Tawny and Trent were together.

Lilah's hand slips into mine, her touch comforting me, reminding me of our bond. I don't move. Don't do anything other than squeeze her hand in a silent thank you.

Minutes tick by as we watch Tawny's body, fingers, and limbs turn to ash. Whatever Kylest did causes it to burn faster than normal. Tawny doesn't get a typical shifter send-off. She gets nothing at all. I hope what my mom said holds true. I hope her soul goes to a place which tortures her in the afterlife.

After everything is done and there are zero remnants

of what happened, Ky and Raven portal home. Ford and Sienna say goodbye and leave as well. I keep my hand in Lilah's and walk to my parents. With one arm, I pull my mom into a hug and hold her for a moment. I've never seen her like this before. So broken and in pain. And I never want to see it again.

Releasing her into my father's arms, he nods then teleports her away. I do the same with Lilah. We're in Duck a second later, in our bedroom.

It's there, in the quiet of the room, where the bed I share with my mate is and the sounds of the ocean as our backdrop, that I crumble and cry. Lilah catches me before I hit the ground and moves us to the bed.

Lilah holds me for hours as I let everything out. Losing Trent. How close I came to losing her. The despair my mom is in. So much pain today. So much agony. There's one person who doesn't know about what happened yet—my cousin, Genevieve. I have no doubt my mom will be the one to deliver the news. They were always close.

Gen lives in Italy as well, though not along the coast near my parents. My heart breaks for her. I can't imagine losing my brother. We're going to be there for Gen, though. All of us. Whatever she needs, we'll provide. We'll soothe her and wrap her in the love of our family.

Lilah and I lie in bed for hours before my stomach growls. I can't even believe I'm hungry. It's then I remember I need to feed. My body is slightly weak and completely exhausted.

Lilah rolls to her back and brings me over her. She cocks her head to the side, offering me what I need. I look into her eyes. It's in them I see more love and devotion than I ever thought possible. I don't need to read her mind to understand how she feels for me. It's powerful and something I'm grateful for.

My fangs descend as my eyes drop to her pulse point. The sound of her blood coursing through her veins becomes music to my ears as I dip my head and pierce her flesh.

The first pull of her blood into my body has me moaning and every part of me filling with lust. The second pull has me grinding on top of her, pressing against her, showing her just how much I want her. The third pull finds us both naked, no clothes separating us, thanks to my female's magic. And the fourth pull has us joining together, connecting in a way only mates truly can.

# CHAPTER TWENTY-EIGHT

## *Lilah*

**THE DAYS FOLLOWING** THE DEATH OF TRENT were filled with more emotion than I'd ever experienced in my life. I thought when my dad left me my heart shattered. I always missed my mom, but I also never knew her. The pain that radiated off every member of the Verascue family nearly brought me to my knees.

The service for Trent was beautiful. He was brought to the land of the Avynwood Pack where there was enough room and privacy to say goodbye. Aries, the pack's alpha, offered to build a platform for Trent's body. Eloise accepted. We stood around him as his body was burned to nothing more than ash. The difference between a Verascue final goodbye and a shifter's is that the ashes of the vampire are put into an urn and stored in a mausoleum that is strictly for the Verascue family. It's on a hilltop in Italy where they own acres surrounding it. No one else can do anything there. It's only for their family.

Genevieve cried as her brother left the earth. I don't have a brother or sister, but I imagine if I ever lost Donovon that I'd feel the same.

Don was in his own pit of hell. His father passed away peacefully in his sleep and his brother continued to lead the pack. It was hard on him to lose his father; even after all they'd been through.

Don stayed with the pack for another month before returning home and overseeing the final reconstruction of his bar. Sol and I were there daily, helping out in whatever way we could until it was finished. Since our home is in Duck, it isn't much of a drive to see Don in Nags Head. Tristin became an employee permanently and another waitress was hired to take my spot, though Don insists she's not as good as I am.

As for me, while I will always love Don and help out whenever he needs me, I'm done bartending. After what I've witnessed since being with Solomon, life's too short. I want to spend every day and night with the male I love.

We're sitting at the new bar, the night before it opens to the public. Donovon only wanted friends and family here tonight. His brother, Alton, and his mate came. A few others from the pack as well. Sol, Ford, Sienna, even Eloise and Seth came out. Ness made an appearance. Jocelyn and Justin are helping with whatever is needed. It wasn't a big group, but it was a tight-knit one.

And man did Don get a kick out of having the entire Verascue clan in his bar. I don't think I've ever seen him smile as wide as he did when Eloise and Seth walked in.

Sol's off to the side talking to his parents when Don walks over to sit next to me at the bar. "Being mated looks good on you," he remarks.

I bump his shoulder with mine. "I never thought I wanted a mate, but I love that idiot with my whole heart."

He smiles. "I know you do, Conni." No matter how many times I tell him he doesn't have to call me by my middle name any longer, he insists on using it. He said it makes him feel special.

The new waitress walks behind the bar to stand next to Tris. Her hair is a dark auburn and flows to her mid-back in soft waves. She's very down to earth and not into appearances. She doesn't wear makeup and has a spattering of freckles across her nose and cheeks. Her eyes are a striking blue and she has a gorgeously curvy body. I don't miss the way Don's eyes track her movements. There's something between them, though I half wonder if she's clued into it yet. I don't see her catch his gaze. She goes about her job, talking with those around us, asking if they need refills. Even Don doesn't get treated any differently.

No regular alcohol for anyone tonight. It's either water, soda, or fae wine. And thanks to Kylest and Raven, we have an entire case of it as a reopening gift. Too bad they couldn't stay for the party.

I send Don a message with my mind. He won't be able to talk back, however, he'll definitely hear me. *"You should ask her on a date."*

He whips his head in my direction, his eyes wide.

Eden is human, though she's aware of our world. She's someone Tristin met while the bar was being rebuilt. From what I heard, they hooked up once, but it was merely that. I can tell the two have become close friends. However, there is no love in either of their eyes.

I focus on Don. *"You won't know if there's something between you two until you try."*

He stands and takes my hand in his to bring me through the back of the bar and outside. Sol cocks an eyebrow at us as we pass by but doesn't move to stop us. If there is one paranormal he can trust me with, it's Donovon.

Once the heavy steel door is shut, Don turns to me.

Sure, if the paranormals inside want to hear our conversation, I'm sure they easily could, but Eden won't be able to. "What are you getting at?" he asks in a rush. "Why would you even bring that up?"

I place my hand on his arm. "I see the way you look at her, Don. That's not lust. It's much more."

He shakes his head. "I can't go there with her. She's my employee."

I chuckle. "Since when do those rules apply in our world?"

"She's not one of us."

I shrug. "She could be if she's your mate. Have you touched her yet? Have your hands brushed together? Anything?"

He shakes his head. "I won't. I'm not ready for that. Not after losing my dad and seeing how distraught my mom was. What if I find my mate and lose them the same way?"

"Your dad lived a long, full life. Any of us would be very fortunate to have the same. Don't sit back and wait because you're afraid. Trust me. I would know." I smile.

"She's too good for me, Conni. I'm a bear shifter. Our world is full of violence. I don't want to bring her into that."

"You already did by having her work for you. Her feet are half planted in the human world and half in the paranormal one. Give it a chance. All you have to do is brush your skin against hers in passing to find out if she's something more than an employee to you."

He ducks his head. "There's something about her that draws me in. I can't explain it."

"You don't have to. I understand completely. That's how I feel about Solomon."

Don rubs the back of his neck. "I'm not sure I can do it."

Tipping his face up so he's forced to look at me, I ask, "Would it be better never to know? Would it be better for her to find someone else and spend her life with them? Another paranormal or a human? Could a human protect her as you can?"

Don growls and his eyes flash ruby red. "No one will lay a hand on what's mine."

I pat his arm, not for one second afraid of him. "That's what I thought. After we leave tonight, I want you to talk to her. Ask her out. Touch her freaking hand, Don. If she feels those sparks, she'll be unable to resist the pull. She'll know she's yours."

"I don't want to force her into anything."

"You won't. Even if she feels the sparks, the decision will always be hers to make. You would never force someone to be with you. But if it's true and she's your mate, you'll get to show her just how amazing you are. And this world we live in, it's not all bad. There are many wonderful things you can open her eyes to. Plus, you'll have Sol, Tris, and me there whenever you need us."

He reaches out and pulls me into a tight embrace. "I don't know what I'd do without you. You're like my sister, but you're also my best friend. I love you, Conni."

I grip him hard but not to the point I'll hurt him. He might be a big bear shifter, but I have Verascue vampire strength. "I love you, too."

The back door to the bar opens and Sol pops his head out. He sees Don and me hugging and smirks. "If you wanted a threesome, kitten, all you had to do was ask."

Don releases me and lets out a shaky laugh. Our conversation affected him more than I thought it would. "I may be envious of your family's power, Solomon, but I draw the line at seeing you naked."

Sol kicks the door all the way open, relaxes against the doorframe, and crosses his arms. "Come on, big boy. Admit it. You want to see what I'm packing. I've got enough stamina to go well into the night." I roll my eyes, even though he's telling the truth. I can't believe how many nights he's completely wrung me out.

Don walks over and clasps him on the shoulder. "Sorry to break it to you, but you're not my type."

Sol scoffs, "I'm everyone's type. The problem is, you've never let a vampire drink from you. More precisely, me. Once you've had a Verascue drink your blood, you'll never want anyone else. One bite from me will give you more pleasure than any other paranormal ever will."

"I'll take your word for it. Now if you'll excuse me, I have people inside I need to talk with."

Sol looks at him for a beat then nods while smiling wide. "Yeah, you do."

Don groans. "Could you stop reading my mind?"

"Where would the fun be in that? I have to be sure you and my kitten are only friends." There's nothing between Don and me, but he's using it to cover up his concern for my friend. Sol may appear flippant to most, but he has a heart of gold and is very protective of those in his inner circle, which now includes Donovon.

Don goes inside, leaving Sol and me alone. I step up to him and he loops his arm around my waist to hold me. "There's someone inside who wants to see you," he says.

"Who?" I've only been out here a few minutes and we weren't expecting anyone else.

"Your father."

My legs go weak, but Sol is there and doesn't let me fall. "Wh-what? He's here? Inside?"

Sol nods. "I didn't tell him you'd talk to him. I wanted

to give you the choice to leave if you chose to. There's nothing you have to do. We can go right now."

"Did he say why he's here?"

Sol shakes his head. "I read his mind, though. He heard what happened to us. He's aware we're mated and how Tawny tried to kill you. He wants to see with his own eyes that you're okay."

"He could have come sooner!" I yell. There's no doubt in my mind he and everyone in the bar heard me.

Sol lifts his hand to gently run his fingers over my cheek. "He was in Austria saying goodbye to a female. She wasn't his mate, but he cared deeply for her. And she died birthing their son."

I gasp as tears immediately form in my eyes. He had to go through it again. I might hate him for what he did to me, but I would never want him to lose someone he cared about a second time, especially during childbirth. "The baby?" I ask.

"He's with him inside. Mom's quite taken with him and hasn't given him back since your dad showed up. She's also not too happy with him, but the baby is buffering her rage."

I laugh through unshed tears and blink them back. Sol's family is looking out for me. "Let's go inside. I want to see him. I'm not sure for how long, but I want to at least lay my eyes on him and meet my brother."

Sol nods and takes my hand in his. Together we go back inside. I'm two steps into the open area when I come to a complete stop. The male in front of me is exactly how I remember him. Tall with brown hair and eyes the same color as mine. I have his straight nose as well. The moment he sees me, tears well in his eyes. He steps forward and my body immediately tenses. He takes notice and stops.

"Lilah," he whispers. "You've grown into a beautiful

female."

I take a moment to read his mind. There's so much remorse there. So much he wants to say but he's holding back, afraid of how I'll react. I rapidly shift through his memories and see how he never forgot about me. He thought I wouldn't want him back in my life, so he stayed away. Until he had Chase, his son.

A tear spills over and runs down his cheek. "I couldn't let him go." He knows enough to realize I was reading his mind. "The biggest regret of my life was not raising you. So I'm here, with your brother, and I want you to know him. You don't have to talk to me, but I want you in his life. We're here for good, Lilah."

His words cause my own tears to reform. I want to be angry. I want to scream at him for what he did to me. For how he made me not want to trust anyone. For how he left me when I needed him most. But then I remember what I've been through since I met Sol. How our lives can end in a moment, regardless if we're immortal or not. I remember the look on everyone's faces as they said goodbye to Trent.

There's no more room for anger in my life. I can't deal with it anymore. While I might not forgive my father, I don't want to push him from my life either. Especially when I have a new brother. I want to see him grow.

"Can I… Can I hold him?" I ask.

He nods and turns. Eloise walks over and instead of bringing Chase to me, she hands him to my father. He doesn't move but waits for me to approach him. I do so cautiously and gently take the little boy from him.

Once in my arms, a smile brightens my face as I peer down into the most gorgeous slate blue eyes I've ever seen. Chase kicks his feet and reaches for my hair as it hangs down around us. This is my brother. He can't be more than a month old.

Sol comes up behind me and wraps his arms around my waist as he peers over my shoulder. "He's beautiful."

There, in the bar that feels like a second home, with a room full of people I love, I'm finally at peace. I have my mate, a brother I'm so happy to meet, and a new family. There's nowhere else in the world I'd rather be.

# Epilogue

## *Solomon*

*...Two Months Later*

**I STIR IN BED AND REACH** OVER FOR MY MATE. She's nuzzled up behind me as I turn, and my hand instinctively searches for her stomach. The baby bump is very small, but it's there, nonetheless. Inside my gorgeous mate is our child—a Verascue of our own making.

Lilah curls up against me, her face buries in my neck. She settles and lets out a contented sigh. There's nothing better than this. Nothing more I could have ever dreamed of. Lilah is my entire world, and I have so much love to give the child within her. I can't wait to spoil him or her rotten.

Lilah's foot touches mine and I flex my sole to caress it then freeze. What the fate? Why is there hair on her foot? I would have noticed if she stopped shaving.

Pushing the foot a little more, I nudge it out of the way so I can trail mine up the leg attached to the hairy foot. More hair. Course hair. What the...?

I prop myself up on my elbow, careful not to disturb my mate and blink a few times in the darkened room while my eyes focus. When they do, I see a body down by my feet.

Immediately, I shoot out of bed and run to the end. I grip the muscular leg of the male in our bed and whip him to the floor. He lands in a hard thud and groans. I'm hovering over him in an instant; my fangs descend as I ready myself to end his life.

"What gives, bestie?" The voice is familiar.

"Wake?"

He looks up and smiles. "Who else would it be?"

"Fate if I know. Why are you in my bed?"

"The babies won't let me sleep. It never ends."

"So, you left Paige there to handle them alone?" I scoff. "Some male you are."

"Nope, I'm here, too," Paige pipes up from the bed. "Aries and Cassie have the girls."

My head snaps over to her, and it's then I realize she's not the only one in my bed with my mate. There are four other shapes.

"All right. Roll call!" I yell. Everyone needs to announce themselves. If I'm going to sleep with other paranormals in my bed, they better tell me who they are.

My request is met with groans and curse words. Ari lifts her head, her long, dark hair falling around her face. "I'm here with Rion. Ford is on the other side of me and Sienna is next to him. That's it. Eight paranormals in a bed. Well, six since you and Wake are over there."

"How freaking big is my bed? I can't believe everyone fits?"

"We're packed in here like sardines, brother," Ford says with a yawn. "Now shut up or get out of the room. It's the middle of the night and I'm exhausted."

"Why are you all in my bed?" I yell. "I was sleeping very well with my mate and now we can't even move."

Wake stands and smirks. That freaking smirk. He learned it from Ford and me. We're clearly spending too much time together. "Paybacks suck, bestie. Now get in the bed and love on us," he says with outstretched arms.

I shove him. "Get away from me. Go home and take your mate with you."

He doesn't relent and comes right up to me to wrap his arms around my waist and put his head on my shoulder. "Mmm, this is nice."

"What is going on right now? Am I dreaming?"

"No dream," Lilah mutters. "Lots of love. You're not throwing anyone out." She yawns and tucks her hand under the pillow cradling her head. I can't get rid of anyone now. Not when she's so peaceful.

I sigh and extract Wake from me. He climbs back into bed and spoons Paige as I go to the edge of my side and lie down. Reaching for Lilah, I pull her into my chest and kiss the top of her head.

*"Love you, kitten,"* I send to her.

*"Love you, too."*

I can't be mad about everyone being here. As much as I might love space to stretch, these paranormals are my family. I would give my life for any one of them. And here they are showing my mate and me the same love I've given them. Okay, so I might not have always shown it in the best way, but they each know how much I care for them. It's not always with words. Sometimes I show with actions and that's okay.

Family isn't just those who share your blood. It's those in your life who've proven to stand by you, to always be there, and weather any storm that comes your way. They don't give up when you're in a bad mood or when you yell. They remain a solid figure you can depend on in good times and in bad. They hold you through your tears and celebrate your joys with you. They're every single paranormal in this room and they're mine.

Regardless of how old we are, our lives are only beginning. We have a long time to be with one another, and we'll do just that—spend our lives as one big, happy family.

Want more of Michelle Dare's paranormals? Next up is A Very Avynwood Christmas! Ford and Solomon are sure to get you in the holiday spirit. If you haven't read Ariane and Orion's story yet, you can start with The Ash Moon. Stay up to date by joining Michelle's reader group on Facebook or by signing up for her newsletter.

Facebook Reader Group:
https://www.facebook.com/groups/daresdivas/

Newsletter Sign-Up:
http://bit.ly/2vBpt9x

# Other Books by Michelle Dare

**Young Adult Titles**

**The Ariane Trilogy**

The Ash Moon

The Somber Call

The Crucial Shift

********

**The Paranormals of Avynwood Series**

Wake's Claim

Ford's Fate

Kylest's Reign

Solomon's Surrender

A Very Avynwood Christmas

**Adult Titles**

**The Iridescent Realm Series**

The Azure Kingdom

The Pine Forest

The Fuchsia Lakes

********

**The Arrow Falls Series**

Where I End

Where I Am

****

**The Salvation Series**

My Salvation

My Redemption

****

**The Heiress Series**

Persuading Him

Needing Him

Adoring Her

****

**The Ray Point Series**

Floating

****

**The Vault Series**

Uncuffed

Unreserved

****

**Standalones**

Daylight Follows

Christmas on the Rocks

The Unattainable Chief

Pleasurable Business

Her Forbidden Fantasy

Michelle Dare is a romance author. Her stories range from sweet to sinful and from new adult to fantasy. There aren't enough hours in the day for her to write all of the story ideas in her head. When not writing or reading, she's a wife and mom living in eastern Pennsylvania. One day she hopes to be writing from a beach where she will never have to see snow or be cold again.

https://www.michelledare.com/

Made in the USA
Columbia, SC
17 May 2021

38089435R00140